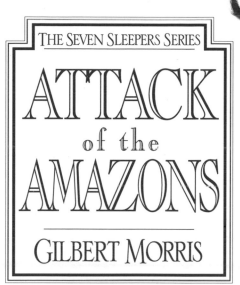

THE SEVEN SLEEPERS SERIES

ATTACK
of the
AMAZONS

GILBERT MORRIS

MOODY PRESS
CHICAGO

SA PL

©1996 by
GILBERT MORRIS

ISBN: 0-8024-3691-9

7 9 10 8 6

Printed in the United States of America

To Leah Workman—
a sweet girl indeed!

Contents

1

Happy Birthday—I Think!

Ow! Will you get your big foot off me, Josh!"

Sarah Collingwood jerked her foot out from under the heavy weight that had descended on it, and shoved Josh Adams away. "Don't stand so close, will you!"

Josh Adams blinked into the murky darkness. "Well, I couldn't help it," he said. "Besides, why are you standing so close to *me?*"

"Why, she's got a crush on you, Josh. Didn't you know that?"

The voice came from somewhere across the darkened room, and the Southern twang identified it as belonging to Bob Lee Jackson, better known to his friends as Reb. He chuckled. "I don't know why we have to go to all this trouble for old Dave. Just for a little old thing like a birthday."

"It's his *seventeenth* birthday, that's why!"

That voice came from another far corner. Jake Garfield started to add something else but then said, "Quiet! I think I hear him coming."

Josh heard footsteps approaching the door, and he held his breath until it opened. For a moment there was silence.

Then, when the young man who had come inside turned on the light, all of them shouted at the top of their lungs, "Happy birthday! Happy birthday, Dave!"

"Hey, what's going—" Dave Cooper could not say more, for suddenly he was surrounded by the six other teenagers, who lunged from their positions, beat him on the back, and shook his hand.

Sarah ruffled his hair so that it fell down into his eyes.

"Hey, cut it out, will you? You want to kill a fella?"

"You only have one seventeenth birthday," Josh said, giving him a hard clip on the shoulder with his fist. "You better make the best of it." Then he said, "All right, you guys, step back and give him a little air. After all, he's a senior citizen now, you know. We have to be careful of our elders. Old Dave is getting along in years."

The subject looked anything but elderly. Dave was exactly six feet tall and well-built. He had yellow hair and blue eyes, and his tan gave him an outdoors look. He grinned at Josh. "That's right! Have a little respect for us old folks."

Abbey Roberts said, "Back in Oldworld we used to spank people on their birthday. One lick for every year old they were."

"Yeah, you go ahead, Abbey." The speaker was a small black boy whose full name was Gregory Randolph Washington Jones. This would have been tiresome to say, so he was known simply as Wash. He had large eyes, and his teeth shown brightly against the blackness of his skin. He nudged Abbey with an elbow. "Go on. You start."

Abbey, at fifteen, had blonde hair and blue eyes and a perfectly shaped mouth. Now she pouted rather prettily. "He's too big. I'll let you guys take care of that, but I will wish him happy birthday like *this*—" She pulled Dave's head down and gave him a kiss on the cheek. Then she said, "Now you, Sarah."

Sarah Collingwood was sixteen. She was small, graceful, and had brown eyes and black hair. Quickly she slipped over and kissed Dave's other cheek. "And now, you guys can give him that spanking anytime you want to."

"We'll take care of that later," Reb said. "Let's give him his presents before we get on with that little ceremony."

Reb was lanky and muscular at six feet one. He had light blue eyes and sun-bleached hair. He was known to give a Rebel yell when he got excited, and now his eyes shown with fun as he said, "Birthday gift!" and shoved a package at Dave.

Self-consciously Dave took the present, muttering, "You guys shouldn't have done this."

"Yeah, you don't deserve it," Reb said. "We all agreed on that. Now, go on and open your presents."

Dave opened the bulky package, and when the paper was ripped away, he looked up and grinned. "Hey, Reb! These are the eelskin boots that I wanted so much. I don't know how you paid for these!" He rubbed their shiny surface. "But thanks. Just what I wanted."

"Well, here you are," Josh said, thrusting a small package at him. This proved to be a razor-edged knife with a bone handle and a black leather sheath that mounted on the belt. "Be careful you don't cut yourself on it—" Josh grinned "—and don't let Jake borrow it. You know how he dulls a knife."

Jake Garfield was much shorter than Reb or Josh or Dave. He had a head of flaming red hair, his brown eyes were sharp, and he had a mind that worked constantly. He ignored Josh's remark and handed Dave a plain brown-paper parcel. "Didn't have time for fancy wrapping paper," he mumbled.

Everyone watched as Dave unwrapped the gift, for Jake was the most innovative of the Seven Sleepers. He loved to invent things, and he watched carefully as Dave took off the paper.

9

"Well, I sure appreciate it," Dave said, puzzlement in his blue eyes, "but what is it?"

"Just push that little button on the side and you'll see."

Cautiously Dave turned over the small black object. It was less than an inch thick, about two inches wide, and three or four inches long. Its smooth case was broken only by one small button. "It won't blow up, will it?" he asked.

"Just push the button," Jake repeated.

Dave held the box at arm's length—he was aware that some of Jake's inventions were rather scary—and pressed the button.

Instantly a high-pitched howl nearly deafened them all.

Dave threw the box across the room and covered his ears. The rest of the Sleepers did the same, and it was Jake who scrambled across the floor and shut off the noise by pushing the button again. He turned his bright eyes on Dave and nodded. "Well, how'd you like that?"

"Wonderful!" Dave exclaimed, removing his hands from his ears. "Maybe I'll be able to hear again in a week or two. What's it for?"

"Why, if somebody jumps out and starts to mug you, you just push the button. It'll scare the waddle out of them."

"It'll sure deafen them," Josh said ruefully. He shook his head and grinned at Jake, for it was just the sort of thing that Jake would do.

Sarah presented her gift, a shirt that she had made herself out of some very soft blue material. "If it's too big, I can take it up," she said anxiously.

Dave held up the shirt, admired it, and smiled at her. "It looks great, Sarah. Thanks a lot."

Then Wash stepped up. "Here. Try this on for size." His gift proved to be a beautifully constructed snakeskin belt, which Dave liked exceedingly and said so.

Abbey's gift was even larger than Reb's, and her eyes glinted as she gave it to Dave and watched him open it.

It was a fawn-colored suede hat—much like the kind Australians wore back in Oldworld. It had one side pinned up, and he put it on at once. "Just a fit," he said. He looked around for a mirror and saw none. "How do I look?"

"You look like Crocodile Dundee," Josh said cheerfully. "Now, let's have the cake. That's all the presents you get."

Abbey and Sarah had made a huge chocolate cake—Dave's favorite—and he blew out the seventeen candles that they'd set afire.

"You always were windy, Dave," Reb said, as the smoke curled upward. "Now, let's get at that cake."

Abbey served huge slices on plates, and they all sat around eating and talking cheerfully.

As Josh sat down next to Sarah, he looked around and thought, *It doesn't seem like two years since we got blasted out of everything we knew and came to Nuworld.* As he looked at his six friends, memories flashed through Josh's mind, and he was soon lost in thought.

The seven of them had been placed in sleep capsules just before a nuclear bomb devastated the earth. Through the miracle of Dave's father's science, they had slept for many, many years. When they awakened, they discovered themselves on a strange planet. The nuclear war had changed the shape of continents and oceans. Mutations had arisen, so that strange and exotic life forms now roamed the earth.

And they soon learned that there was a war going on, involving a strange figure called Goél, who appeared and disappeared with startling speed. Goél stood for the old values that they had learned to treasure, but he was opposed by sinister forces led by one called the Dark Lord. All of Nuworld was now a battleground, and the Sleepers had thrown themselves into Goél's service without reservation.

Now Sarah leaned over and asked, "What do you think this assembly is about, Josh?" She spoke of a calling together of the leaders of the House of Goél. They had come from strange and distant places all over Nuworld, and all of them were wondering what was to come.

Josh, who was the leader of the Sleepers, stretched out his six-foot frame in his chair. He had grown up very fast and was still a little embarrassed by his tall, gangly shape. He had not filled out yet like Dave and still had not lost some of his adolescent countenance. He had auburn hair, blue eyes, and had always been a shy boy, unsure of himself. He wondered often why Goél had chosen him to be the leader when there were others smarter and stronger. He had learned to cope with this, however, and covered his insecurities with a good imitation of confidence.

"I think it must be something pretty big," he told Sarah. "Goél has never done this before. He's always come to us individually." He scratched his cheek thoughtfully, then took another huge bite of chocolate cake.

The Sleepers had been hundreds of miles away when the summons from Goél came, and they had rushed as fast as they could to the general meeting place.

"It must be trouble," Jake said.

"Why does it have to be trouble?" Abbey asked. "Maybe it's good news."

"You never saw a mob rushing across town to do a good deed," Jake stated flatly. "Anytime we get a call like this, you can bet there's got to be a problem."

"Well, we'll find out in the morning," Dave said. He looked fondly around at his friends. "After all the troubles and hard times we've been through, I guess we ought to be used to difficult things."

Dave looked more like an adult than anyone else in the room, although he was only one year older than some of the others. But as it is with some young men, the year between sixteen and seventeen had brought a maturity that did not come to all. He was broad-shouldered, and his body had filled out with sleek muscles so that he looked like an Olympic swimmer.

"I guess," Dave said, as he put down his empty plate, "whatever Goél says, we'll do it. Sometimes I think we're losing, though—that the Dark Lord is gaining ground so fast that we'll never make it."

"You can't think like that, Dave. None of us can!" Sarah exclaimed. Of all the Sleepers, she, perhaps, had more faith in victory than any of the others, and now she said cheerfully, "Let's get to bed. We might get sent off on a mission to the ice cap tomorrow. Who knows?"

For once the young people had been housed together. The boys had been assigned two rooms, and Abbey and Sarah had a room to themselves. The bathroom was down at the end of the hall, however, and they had to take turns.

While they were waiting, Dave drifted over to Abbey. "I sure like this hat." He put it on again and turned for her inspection. "It looks good, doesn't it?"

"Why don't you let somebody else brag on you, Dave? You're getting downright conceited."

There was such sharpness in Abbey's voice that Dave was surprised. He looked at her and answered in kind. "You're a fine one to be talking!" he snapped. "You spend half your time primping."

"I'm just trying to look nice. I don't see anything wrong with that."

"I don't either. That's why I'm trying on my new hat!" Actually, Dave was still pleased with his birthday party. He changed his tone. "It was awful nice of you and the rest of the gang to do this for me, Abbey," he said. He studied her for a moment, thinking how pretty she was. "You know," he said, "when you grow up, you're going to be some foxy lady."

"When I grow up! I *am* grown up!"

"Fifteen is not grown up."

"I'm almost sixteen. Besides, girls are more mature than boys. Didn't you know that?"

"I don't know who invented that rumor. I never noticed girls being that much smarter."

Abbey, for some reason, was out of sorts. Perhaps she was nervous about the mission. It had taken a terrible experience in the Underworld for her to learn that her beauty was not something to be trusted. She had learned that lesson the hard way—and not completely, perhaps. And if one of the Sleepers could be said to be fearful, she was the one. The others had to constantly keep her cheered up. Now she was upset with Dave.

"Of *course* girls are more mature than boys, and they could run the world better too."

"You're just bossy," Dave said. He settled the hat on his head and tried it at a new angle. "I wish I had a mirror," he muttered, "so I could see what I look like."

He glanced at her. "Women would make a mess of the world if they ran it."

An argument broke out at once, and the two picked at each other until they were really angry.

Sarah came into the room, stopped dead still, and stared at them. "Are you two arguing *again?* What's it about this time?"

Dave reached out and patted Abbey on the head—something he knew always infuriated her. "This child thinks she's grown up. Try to straighten her out, will you, Sarah? And tell her that men are made to take care of women. You know how it is—women are weaker. They need to be cared for."

Furiously, Abbey slapped Dave's hand away. "Get out of here . . . you . . . you immature *man!*"

Dave laughed at her and, turning, left the room.

"Why don't you two stop picking at each other?" Sarah asked in exasperation. "It looks like you'd get tired of fighting all the time."

"He thinks he's so smart—and so grown up!"

"Well, Dave *is* pretty smart," Sarah said calmly, "and he's very grown up. He's big as a man, and he's changed a lot over the past two years. Try to get along with him, won't you, Abbey?" She sighed. "I don't think we can stand you two fussing much more."

Abbey sniffed. "I'd like to be his boss for just about one week! I could really make something out of him." She smiled and tapped her cheek gently with a finger. The smile brought out a dimple, and she nodded. "Yes, I certainly would like to have charge of Mr. David Cooper for a little while!"

2
The Power of Goél

The Seven Sleepers ate a hurried breakfast and joined the other servants of Goél already assembled in the large open space just outside the village where they had spent the night. An enormous crowd had gathered in the bright morning sunlight.

Josh looked around. "This place is as large as a soccer field," he muttered. "And it looks like we'll meet some old friends here."

The crowd was composed of every sort of being that inhabited Nuworld. Some were dwarfs, stocky and sturdy. Some were towering giants. Some had come on foot. Some, like the Sleepers, had come by ship.

The Sleepers met a pair of Gemini twins that they had shared an adventure with, and they had just started to exchange stories when Dave whispered, "Look, there's Goél."

All of them turned to see a man wearing a light gray robe, with the hood thrown back, step up onto a mound where he could be seen by everyone. It was impossible to guess his age. He could have been anywhere between twenty-five and fifty-five. He had smooth, tanned cheeks and a pair of thoughtful brown eyes, well-socketed, and his long brown hair fell back over his robe. There was an athletic strength about him but also a gentleness in his countenance that one could not miss.

He spoke, and his voice was clear and penetrating, so that it carried back to the far reaches of the crowd.

"You're welcome here, one and all," he said and looked around as a slight smile tugged at his lips. "Some of you have come a long distance and are tired. I wish that I could promise you a long rest, but I'm afraid my summons calls you to labors even more arduous than those you have already known."

"Oh, me!" Jake groaned. "I know what that means. Off on another adventure."

"Hush up, Jake," Josh said irritably. "You're always complaining."

"Our task is difficult," Goél continued. "The Dark Lord has spread his venom into every corner of Nuworld. Even now he is assembling an army, the like of which you have never seen. Soon he will have his forces gathered and will throw them against us in one mighty attempt to crush those who believe in the old ways."

A cry went up. "He can't beat us, Goél. Not as long as you're our leader."

Goél smiled as others joined in the encouraging cries. When they died down, he said gently, "It is difficult for a commander to send his soldiers into battle, knowing that some of them will not survive. And I must warn you that in the battle to come, many of you will perish. I know you too well to allow you an opportunity to leave, for you have proved your worth time and time again."

Here, his eyes seemed to rest on the Seven Sleepers—but later Josh found out that every soldier in that mighty group had the same feeling. Somehow Goél had the ability to speak to a large crowd and yet make each member of it feel that he alone was being addressed.

Goél continued to talk of the preparations that had to be made, and they were momentous indeed. He spoke of plans, of weapons that must be formed, of strategy. Finally he said softly, though everyone could hear him, "The enemy thinks only in terms of large armies, and, indeed, he has the numbers at his beck and call. But I tell you that it is not always the largest army that wins. The race is not always to the swift, nor the battle to the strong."

His voice rose then with an authority that caused a thrill to run through Josh. He stood upright and hung on every word.

"And the battles that are to come may well be the kind in which one person or one small group is able to turn the tide from defeat to victory. When you receive your assigned task, it may seem small and unimportant to you, but it is not, I tell you. Every sword counts. Even those who seem unimportant and feeble are worthy in my sight, for the House of Goél is my pride."

The Seven Sleepers joined in the cheers that smote the morning air.

Josh cheered himself almost hoarse, and then, when Goél dismissed them, he turned to Sarah and said, "I never understand who he is or what he is—but he's not like any man I know."

Sarah said thoughtfully, "He's more than a man, Josh. No man could do the things that he does."

The crowd broke up, and the Sleepers headed back to the village where they would await Goél's summons to receive their assignment.

Josh walked along with Sarah. "I think you're right," he said. "There's something so . . . well, so *good* about him, Sarah. Everyone else that I ever met has some flaw." He grinned. "Why, even I myself am not perfect all the time!" But he grew serious at once, saying, "He's all we have to hang on to. We lost everything when we lost our homes and families back in Oldworld, but somehow I know—and this sounds silly—that we'll get them back again some day."

For two days the Sleepers waited for Goél to come to them. They were somewhat impatient—and a little apprehensive. When Goél came, he always sent them into some dangerous adventure. At first this had been exciting. Now they had been at it for two years and were like soldiers who had been on the battle line almost too long.

Jake expressed everyone's feeling when he said, "I don't know how long we can hold together. A fellow can take only so many tough jobs."

The seven were outside, eating the meal that they had rounded up from a local woman. It was composed of some sort of meat that was not as appetizing as it should have been, and Jake stared down at it. "I wonder what this *is*," he said thoughtfully.

"Better not ask," Reb said. He tasted his portion and then shook his head. "One thing, it's not possum. Boy," he said, "I'd sure like to have a mess of possum and sweet taters like I had back home."

"Ugh!" Abbey said. "I can't *imagine* eating a possum. It'd be just like eating a big rat."

Reb was offended. "You just don't know what you're talking about. What we do is, we catch a yearling possum, and then we keep him caged, and we feed him nothing but corn and good stuff for a month. Why, the time you get him all cooked, there ain't nothing better than good possum with some sweet taters and cornbread."

Reb's choice in Southern food turned off some of the Sleepers, but Josh, tasting the meat that was before him, said, "I think possum would be better than this—

although I never tried it." He looked up and set aside his plate. "Here comes Goél."

Instantly the Seven Sleepers got to their feet and stood until Goél came up to them.

He smiled and said, "Sit down—finish your meal."

"Well, would you have some, Goél?" Josh asked timidly. "It's not much."

"Why, yes, I believe I will." He took the plate that Sarah eagerly brought to him, and he ate, seeming to enjoy the food. "Hunger is the best sauce," he said pleasantly.

His eyes went from one to the other, and Abbey supposed that all the others felt as she did—that somehow he had entered into their innermost thoughts. She flushed when she remembered how proud she had been of her good looks, and how Goél had told her long ago, before their first adventure, that she would have to learn how foolish it was to trust in physical beauty. It was still disconcerting to look into his eyes, for he knew everything about her!

Goél began talking about their past and commended them for their fine work. "You have been faithful to me," he said.

"Well," Josh said haltingly, "we haven't always scored a hundred."

"I do not judge my servants by what they accomplish but by what's in their hearts, and your hearts have been through a furnace. I have tried you, my young friends, and found pure gold. I am pleased with my Seven Sleepers."

Abbey felt a sudden flush of pleasure at his words. More than anything else, the Sleepers wanted to please this one whom they did not understand but whom they loved.

Wash said tentatively, "We've been wondering

what's going to happen, Sire." He gave Goél the title that many used. "It doesn't sound too good. I mean, that Dark Lord, he's a bad cat!"

"Yes, he is evil, but with servants like you, Wash, I do not fear for the House of Goél." He smiled as pleasure spread over the small boy's face, then Goél grew serious. "Now I have an assignment for you. It will be difficult, but I know that you will do your best—"

Jake suddenly piped up. "Why don't you just use your power and smash that old Dark Lord?" he demanded. "You could do it. Just step on him like a cockroach!"

Goél held the small boy by the power of his look and said softly, "But if I did that, it would mean that you and the others in this world would have no freedom. You are free to choose—that is the glory of what you are. What would it be like if you had no choices to make?"

Dave straightened up. "Why, we'd be a race of robots."

"Exactly, David, and robots can give no pleasure to me. It is when you are free to choose for me or against me—and you choose me against all odds—that is what pleases me."

Abbey and the other Sleepers listened, soaking up his words as he spoke of love. He seemed to be asking them for more than their service. It was strange that a being like Goél would beg for love, but that was what he appeared to be doing.

"My servants in this world must survive by one thing—their love for me. Nothing else means more than your love for me and for one another. Love is the most powerful force in this universe."

Then Goél said, "Now it is time for your assignment." He pulled a small parchment out of his cloak.

"Here is a map. Guard it well. Memorize it, so that if it gets lost you can have it in your minds, each of you."

"Where are we going, Goél?"

"This may seem to you a minor mission, but I want you to go to a small nation—a tribe—far away. The tribe is called the Tribe of Fedor."

"Do they know about you, Goél, or are they under the power of the Dark Lord?"

"The Dark Lord is reaching out in their direction. He has no stronghold there yet, but he will if the people there do not learn how dangerous he is." His face grew stern, and his eyes seemed to flash with anger. "You must meet the enemy there on his own ground."

"Will there be real fightin'?" Reb asked with some excitement. He was a combative young man and very good with any kind of weapon.

"There will be physical battle, but, my son, you must remember that the greatest weapon is not a sword or a lance but love."

Reb looked chagrined and seemed to draw his head back into his shoulders. "I reckon so," he muttered, but he appeared to be unconvinced.

"To fight is your nature, my son, and I need strong arms such as yours—but love is more powerful than anything else. You must win the minds and the hearts of these people. They are deceived about many things. Be patient. You *can* win them, but they are in darkness and are blind and need the light."

For some time Goél spoke about their mission, but he gave no specific instructions. "Simply tell them that Goél brings joy and peace to men, while the Dark Lord brings misery and slavery."

Goél stood then and went to each one of them, clasping their hands, and Abbey thought his smile seemed to pour strength into them.

"I will come to you when you need me, as always," he said. "But sometimes in the darkness and difficulties you will face, you will not see me. That is when you must simply believe that Goél loves you and will not ever leave you."

He turned and walked away quickly, headed purposefully toward another group.

Josh said slowly, "Well, nothing much has changed. It's another hard assignment." But then, looking around at the solemn faces, he said, "Let's get ourselves geared up. We've got a job to do."

3
Old Friends

Once their assignment had been received, the Sleepers threw themselves into a frenzy of activity. The journey they had to make would be arduous and cover great distances. They were experienced enough by this time to handle such things, but such a trip took great preparation.

Reb took it upon himself to check the weapons, for they were his delight. Nuworld had not developed explosives, so the weapons were a primitive kind— swords, knives, bows, and spears. Spears were awkward, but all of the Sleepers had become good archers. Dave and Reb and Sarah were experts. In the matter of swords, Josh was perhaps the best fencer of all.

Abbey and Sarah were usually in charge of food and were, of course, aware that it was impossible to carry enough. They did take as much dried foodstuff as they could and a supply of coffee and tea. The cooking vessels themselves had to be light and easily carried, for they had learned, to their discomfort, how heavy a pack could get after a ten-hour hike.

Reb got into an argument with Dave over his lariat. The cowboy was an expert roper and saw the lariat as a necessary part of his equipment.

"We need to get rid of every spare ounce, Reb. You won't need that rope where we're going."

"And how do you know that?" Reb demanded. "It came in pretty handy when I roped that there dinosaur back in the land of the caves, didn't it?" He referred to an adventure they had had where prehistoric dinosaurs still roamed a portion of Nuworld. "I'm carrying this rope, even if I have to leave some of my grub behind." Reb would not listen to any arguments, and finally it went into his pack along with the rest of his gear.

The big argument came when Dave discovered that Abbey was putting a bag that did not look like standard equipment into her pack. "What's *that?*" he asked suspiciously.

"None of your business!" Abbey flushed. "Something for my personal use."

"I know what it is," Dave accused. "It's cosmetics, isn't it? Lipstick and stuff like that."

"Well, what if it is?"

"You aren't going to any fancy parties. You don't need that stuff."

"You mind your own business, Dave Cooper!"

"It'll be my business if you drop, carrying a hundred pounds of cosmetics, and I have to carry you and your pack too."

Abbey's eyes flashed. She really made a pretty picture as she stood before him, her hands on her hips. "I don't think you've ever had to carry me, have you?"

"There's always a first time."

The argument went on for some time, and finally Abbey said, "I'm taking this little bag, and that's all there is to it." She shoved the bag inside her pack, fastened it down with the leather thongs, and turned to face him again. "You just mind your own business, Dave Cooper. Like I've told you, women can do better than men if they just have the chance."

Josh broke up the argument by saying, "Let her carry it if she wants to, Dave. That's her problem. Come on—it's time to start."

They left the village and made their way in a day's

journey to the seacoast. A ship was anchored in the small harbor, its sails furled.

"There's Captain Daybright's ship, waiting for us!" Wash said excitedly.

They hurried down to the harbor, where the first person they saw was Captain Ryland Daybright himself. He gave them a loud hello and then called back to the ship. "Dawn, they're here! Come ashore."

As the Sleepers hurried forward to greet the tall, blond-headed captain, who looked more or less like one of the old-time Vikings, Sarah was looking at the young woman who hurried down a plank to the dock. "Dawn!" she said and ran to give her friend a hug.

Dawn was the captain's new bride. The two had been on one of the Sleepers' adventures in a land inhabited by giants. She had been a haughty girl, the daughter of a wealthy man, and Daybright had been a poor seaman. But they had fallen in love after many arguments, and now they made an attractive couple. Dawn was a small girl with blonde hair and strangely shaded green eyes.

"Well, ready for another adventure?" Daybright asked cheerfully.

"I hope we don't get messed up with another bunch of giants," Wash said dolefully. "I don't need any more of that."

"What's our destination?" Ryland asked.

"It's right here. We're going to a tribe at this spot." Josh unfolded the map, and the captain looked at it quickly.

Daybright's brow furrowed, and his eyes grew serious. "I know the coast but not what's inland. Some strange stories about it. It's no place to go for a nice little vacation."

"I wish there was someplace on Nuworld like

Disneyland," Jake said suddenly. "Where we could just go and have fun. Everywhere we go here, we get thrown in jail, or somebody tries to kill us."

"Aw, Jake, you'd complain if they hung you with new rope," Reb sniffed. "Now, me, I kind of like a little adventure."

This was true. In the land known as Camelot, Reb had found adventure enough. The inhabitants there still were knights and princesses, and Reb had become an expert jouster. It was his hope and dream to go back there someday.

Now he said hopefully, "Maybe there'll be some knights in this place."

Captain Daybright shook his head. "I don't think you'll find anything quite that civilized. "Well, come on. Get aboard. We've got to catch the tide."

The voyage was a pleasure to most of the Sleepers. Wash got seasick for the first two days, but Reb took good care of him—and when he recovered, the small black boy joined in the activities with the others.

This included standing at the rail and watching for the whales that seemed to abound in this part of Nuworld. The monstrous creatures, larger than the ship itself, would surface and then roll slowly, their full length, slapping the water with a tremendous crash of their fan-shaped tails.

"Why do they do that, do you suppose?" Wash asked Captain Daybright.

"I don't know. Maybe it's fun, or maybe it's just the way they get from one place to another. Whales aren't fish, you know."

"They're not?" Wash said in surprise. "They look like fish to me."

"No, they're air breathers. They can stay under for

a long time, but they have to come up. See that spout?" He pointed to where what looked like a small island had appeared. Suddenly a geyser of water blew into the air. "That's what they do. Come up and blow all that water out and take in air. Then they go way down deep again. Magnificent creatures, aren't they?"

"They're big enough to swallow people," Jake muttered.

Reb nodded. "I expect so. They're big enough to swallow just about anything,"

The sleepers found fun in fishing too—throwing lines over the side, never knowing what they would dredge up. Some of the things they caught were hideous.

"Why, that even looks worse than a possum," Dave said, teasing Reb. The young Southerner had pulled in an awful-looking specimen.

Reb shook his head. "It doesn't look too good, does it? I'd hate to eat this thing." He threw it overboard. "Reckon somebody might like to eat it, but not me."

They did catch fish that were good to eat, and one night at supper Josh said, "We'd better enjoy this good food. I don't know what we'll eat when we get inland."

"Probably monkeys," Jake said solemnly.

"Monkeys!" Abbey looked up with a startled expression. "Not me. I'm not eating a monkey."

"Aw, they're not bad," Daybright said, with a wink at Josh.

"You never ate a monkey," his bride said.

"Well, I've eaten stuff when I didn't know exactly what it was. When you've been in some of the places I've been, you just carry lots of hot sauce and put it over whatever they feed you—and don't ask questions. That'd be a good idea. I've got plenty of it on board," he told the Sleepers.

"I think we'll take you up on that," Josh said. "We'll have to take what they give us. It offends primitive people if you don't eat what they do."

Daybright leaned back in his chair. He had broad shoulders, and his white teeth shone against his tan complexion in a most attractive way. "I think I'd like to go with you on this trip," he said. "It sounds like a real adventure."

Dawn reached over and rapped him on the side of the head. "You're not going anywhere."

Ryland Daybright shrugged and winked at Dave. "You know how it is when you get married, you guys. A man's life is not his own. But," he said, "I do have a special reason for staying pretty close to home."

Sarah glanced at Dawn, who flushed under her gaze. "I'll bet I know," Sarah said with a smile. "There's going to be a little Daybright."

"Yes," Dawn said, and all smiled. "Isn't that exciting?"

It was exciting enough for the two girls, who got together with Dawn and talked enthusiastically about babies and baby clothes.

Daybright and the boys listened for a while, then he drew them topside, where he stood in the bow, pointing. "You can't see it, but this land you're going to lies right out there. I'd like to go, but wifey says no."

They stood on deck for a long time, looking into the distance.

After the evening meal—which was composed of fish, as usual, and some dried vegetables—Abbey took a walk on deck. Dave found her leaning over the rail, peering out into the twilight. The sun was setting on the horizon—a huge red ball that had half disappeared into the green waters.

"You almost expect that thing to sizzle when it goes into the water like that, don't you, Abbey?" he said.

"It's beautiful."

Dave studied the crimson circle that did, indeed, seem to be easing down into the flat horizon. "I guess so," he said. He turned to face her and said, "I think girls notice things like that more than most guys do."

Abbey did not answer, but she inwardly agreed. As they talked, she could not help but think how fine-looking Dave was. His features were as clean-cut as any Hollywood movie star's, and she thought suddenly, *If we were back in Oldworld, he'd have every girl in the place chasing after him.*

Dave seemed to be unaware of her regard and continued leaning on the rail, studying the horizon. Then unfortunately, he made a chance remark. "We ought to make good time if you girls don't slow us up once we get into the jungle."

Instantly Abbey's eyes snapped. "I remember the time when we were in the desert and you got sick. Then we had to wait until you got well. It took all Sarah and I could do to take care of you. You were just like a big baby! All men are babies when they get sick."

Dave flushed. "Well," he said defensively, "it wasn't my fault. Anybody can get sick."

Abbey goaded him. "You were just like a two year old—crying and complaining all the time."

"I was not!" Dave said angrily.

The argument did not end until the two finally left the deck, headed in different directions.

Unknown to Dave and Abbey, Sarah and Josh were seated on the upper part of the ship's structure, watching the sunset. When Dave and Abbey began talking, Sarah had whispered, "We ought not to be eavesdropping."

"I know, but we're going to, aren't we?" Josh's eyes sparkled, and he added, "I love to eavesdrop! It's always been a hobby of mine."

"You're just awful, Josh Adams."

"Yes, I know, but you're going to help me be awful, aren't you? Listen—they're getting into another fight."

The pair sat there listening as Abbey and Dave argued and then finally broke away from each other. When they had disappeared, Sarah said regretfully, "That's such a shame the way they fight all the time."

"Oh, I don't know. It gives them something to do. It keeps them from getting bored."

"It's not right, Josh, and you know it."

Josh leaned back against the rail and stretched out his long legs. He was barefoot and wearing a pair of cutoffs, and the breeze felt good on his bare legs. "I guess you're right," he said. "I remember a few of the fights *we've* had." He grinned down at her. "They weren't any fun. I was always glad when they were over."

"So was I." Sarah smiled back. She was wearing shorts too and a green blouse made of some sort of soft material. "We've always been good friends, haven't we? Even back in Oldworld."

"Well, I wasn't very nice to you back then," Josh reflected. "I remember when I met you. I was real impressed, but I didn't want to show it."

Sarah laughed suddenly, her laughter sounding light and tinkling on the air. "You certainly didn't show it! You were a real snob, and I was so scared and alone."

Josh reached over and took her hand. "I'm sorry about that. I've told you before, but I'll tell you again."

Sarah seemed pleased. She squeezed his hand. "Oh, well, girls are just more romantic. Why, look at Dave and Abbey—they'll probably fall in love."

"Those two? They fight like cats and dogs."

"That's the way it always is. Haven't you ever read any romances? The course of true love never runs smooth."

"Well, theirs doesn't, that's for sure." Josh was conscious of Sarah's soft hand in his, and it embarrassed him. Suddenly he pulled his own back. "I don't know. It seems like that's not quite right."

"And don't you remember how Captain Daybright and Dawn fought so much? You would've thought they hated each other." She nodded firmly. "I knew right away they were going to fall in love."

"Then I guess you and I will never fall in love. We don't fight that much."

This seemed to displease her. She got up and said, "Good night, Josh. You have no romance in your soul."

Josh sat there dumbly, wondering what he had done. Finally he shook his head and said, "I guess I'll never learn to understand women if I live to be a hundred years old!"

4
Jungle Trek

I guess we're ready," Josh announced. He glanced up at the ship, which had nudged into the sandy beach, and said wistfully, "We may not see you again for a long time. Wish us luck."

Captain Daybright and Dawn had helped unload their supplies and now stood looking at the Sleepers with affection. "We'll wait here for you. I wish I were going along, but you'll be all right," Daybright said. He went around shaking hands with each of them.

Dawn followed his example, giving each a hug. When she had embraced the last one, she stepped back and said, "It's very dangerous in there. I wish you didn't have to go."

"It'll be all right," Dave said cheerfully. "We've got plenty of supplies and weapons, and Goél sent us, so how can we miss?"

"That's a good way to look at it." Captain Daybright nodded approval. But he glanced over toward the inland country—far away, low hills rose, humped like elephants—and he frowned, remembering something. "As I told you," he said, "for the first hundred miles, you've got mostly plains. Then the country starts rising until you get to those hills there. After that I don't know much about the country except from old reports I get. It's some pretty thick jungle. You got your machetes?"

"Got 'em," Reb said, pulling his bright, shiny knife from its sheath and brandishing it.

Josh would like to have stayed longer, but looking up at the sun he said, "It's getting late, and I want to make a good start. Good-bye, Captain—good-bye, Dawn."

The Sleepers headed away from the beach.

After they had walked steadily for a while, Josh took one look back. He could just see the top mast of the ship, and it gave him an odd feeling, knowing that they were on their own.

"Are you a little bit worried, Josh?" Sarah asked. She had come up to walk beside him. Her green pack pulled her shoulders back, but she walked strongly, matching him step for step.

"I guess it's always a little hard, going into an unknown country," he admitted, "but we'll be all right. You're not worried, are you?"

"Not as long as you're here to lead us."

Sarah was well aware of his insecurities, Josh thought, and never missed a chance to give him an encouraging word.

"You've led us through some hard times and dangerous places, and you've never failed yet."

Josh flushed, but he was pleased. "I don't know. I've thought several times that Dave ought to be the leader. He's the oldest and the biggest, and I guess he's the strongest too. Except maybe for Reb."

"Goél knew who to put in charge. For a long time Dave was so self-centered," Sarah remembered, "that he couldn't lead anybody. And as for Reb, he's not stable enough. He's bold as a lion and a fine fighter—but a leader has to be able to think ahead, and that's what you do best, Josh."

He smiled and kept his eyes fixed on the rising mounds ahead of them. "I'm glad you think so. It's good

36

to hear you talk like that, anyhow. I get a little—well, a little afraid I can't handle the job sometimes."

"Goél knew what he was doing when he made you the leader."

By the time the sun was falling in the west, everyone was tired.

"This knapsack is cutting my arms off!" Abbey moaned. She looked hot and sweaty.

Dave, walking beside her, reached up and unfastened the flap of her backpack before she could stop him. Plucking out the bag of cosmetics, he grinned. "Let's just throw this away—then it won't hurt so bad."

"You give me that, Dave!" Abbey snatched the bag from him and, reaching awkwardly over her head, stuffed it back into the pack. Then she turned to Josh and said, "Can we stop pretty soon? We've come far enough today."

"I've been looking for some water," Josh said. "You see that line of trees over there? It looks like they might line a creek or a small river. I hope so, anyway."

They all perked up and quickened the pace as they headed for the trees. When they got there, they found that the green growth did indeed border the bank of a beautiful small stream.

"Hey, I bet there's fish in there," Reb said eagerly. "Wash, let's you and me get the lines out. We can run a trotline tonight."

"OK," Wash agreed.

The two quickly got out their fishing gear. While the others set up camp, they staked out a line that ran a hundred yards down the creek. It was a shallow river, and they could wade it while they tied on hooks at five-foot intervals. They had to bait them with dried meat, and Reb frowned. "This isn't very good bait. The first fish we catch, we'll cut him up, and use *him* for bait."

They caught a fine two-pounder within an hour, and soon all the lines were baited.

The sun had gone down, and Josh and Dave had gathered enough wood to make a cheerful fire. The Sleepers gathered around it, cooking one of the fish that Reb had pulled out of the river. The smell of it made everyone's mouth water—and when Sarah divided it up, they all burned their mouths, trying to eat too fast. The fish was white and tender and did not have the strong taste that many fish did.

"Boy, this is good fish!" Reb said. "Not as good as a blue channel cat caught back in Arkansas, but pretty good for Nuworld."

"You might as well stop thinking about Arkansas. It's all gone," Jake said shortly. His own home in New York was gone too, and it sometimes came home to him with a poignant shock that all that he had grown up with was now over. All of them had only memories of Oldworld.

But Jake was basically a cheerful young man, and as he ate, listening to Reb's tall tales about fishing and hunting, he grew more content. Looking around at the faces illuminated by the flickering light of the fire, he thought, *A fellow would go a long way before he'd find friends as good as these.*

"What's the smartest dog you ever had, Reb?" Josh asked.

"Well—" Reb scratched his head thoughtfully, "—I've had plenty of good hounds, but I guess maybe the smartest was Old Blue. Now that was a dog! I didn't know how smart he was until the day Pap sold one of the cows."

He leaned back, picked up another piece of fish, and nibbled at it thoughtfully. "We had three cows, and every day I'd send Old Blue out to bring 'em in. One day Pap sold one of the cows. A fellow came and took her, so I sent Old Blue down that day to get the other two. Well, that dog just wouldn't believe it! He hunted and hunted, and I tried to tell him that Pap had sold one, but he just couldn't seem to understand that there wasn't a third cow." Reb shook his head and looked mournful.

"What did you do?" Sarah asked in a sympathetic tone.

Reb grinned, his blue eyes flashing in the firelight. "Well, I showed him the check we got for that other cow! He was all right then."

A laugh went around the circle, and he said, "Some of you may not believe these stories, but they's actual."

The next morning Josh roused them all before dawn, and as the light began to make a thin white line in the east, they cooked a quick breakfast of bacon, which they ate with a loaf of bread baked in the ship's galley. Then they shrugged into their knapsacks and filled their canteens with fresh water from the stream.

Josh said, "Let's go. We want to make good time today."

They did make good time all morning. First they passed over a plain, very level, with trees in small clumps and crossed from time to time by wandering streams. The land began to rise a little by noon. Then they went down into a small canyon. Scrambling up the other side, they saw what looked like an oasis in the distance.

"I bet there's water over there," Josh said. "Let's go see."

The Sleepers headed toward the mass of trees and

found that a small creek had been dammed up by a rock slide and made a large pool. Throwing off their knapsacks, they washed their faces.

Then Abbey said, "I want to have a bath. Let's go upstream, Sarah."

"All right." Sarah was hot and tired herself, and a dip sounded good.

They followed the creek until they found a deep spot in the shelter of several trees and were soon splashing in the water. Since Abbey had brought soap, they even washed their hair.

As they dressed, Abbey said, "I wish I could go to a beauty shop."

"A beauty shop!" Sarah laughed. "You won't find one of *those* anywhere on Nuworld." Then she turned her head to one side. "Did you hear something, Abbey?"

Abbey was combing her hair, which was long and lustrous and gleaming in the sun. "No, I didn't hear anything. What'd it sound like?"

"I don't know," Sarah said uncertainly. "Oh, I guess it was nothing." She continued brushing her own hair.

The girls had just finished their hairdos when a sudden snorting made them both whirl around.

Abbey let out a small cry. *"Sarah!"*

"Run, Abbey!"

The two girls began running wildly. Sarah cast one look over her shoulder at the huge bull elephant that had appeared from over a ridge and was charging after them. "He's going to catch us!" she cried. She started screaming. "Josh! *Josh!*"

The girls flew alongside the creek, but the elephant, its white tusks curving wickedly and looking as sharp as needles, was gaining on them.

When they came in sight of the boys, Sarah shrieked, "Run, Josh! All of you, run!"

40

Josh had been bathing his feet in the stream. When he saw the girls and an enormous elephant thundering behind them, he yelled, "Cross the creek! That'll slow him down."

Sarah grabbed Abbey's arm, and the girls splashed across the stream, where they jumped behind an outcropping of rock.

The boys took what cover they could behind trees. On the way, Josh grabbed the white shirt that he had washed and hung out to dry. He waved it furiously, hollering at the elephant.

The beast slowed. The shirt took his attention from the girls, and he stopped uncertainly—confused, evidently, by the waving shirt and the shouting.

Seeing this, Josh said, "Everybody—yell as loud as you can."

Instantly every one of the Sleepers began shouting. The other boys pulled off their shirts and waved them from behind the trees.

The elephant swung his head from one side to the other. His ears stood out like huge black flags, and his little reddish eyes stared wildly around.

"Now everybody get quiet," Josh commanded, "and stop waving those shirts."

Immediately there was silence.

The elephant trumpeted but did not seem to know what to do.

Josh stood stock-still, waiting for the elephant to charge. He did not move a muscle, and all the time he was saying, "Goél, help us!"

As if in response to this, the elephant turned, still trumpeting, and retreated.

Nobody stirred until he was out of sight, and then Josh said, "Quick, get your stuff, and let's get out of here!"

Sarah and Abbey splashed back from their hiding place, both of them pale. They grabbed their knapsacks, and the boys threw their gear together. Then everybody sprinted across the stream, looking over their shoulders, but the elephant did not reappear.

"That was a close one," Dave said. He was a little pale too, as were all of them. Glancing at Josh, he said, "That was smart, Josh. I wouldn't have thought of that."

"Josh always thinks fast," Sarah said. She moved closer and held Josh's arm for a moment. "You see," she whispered, when no one could hear, "I told you that you were a natural leader."

"Well, I hope we don't meet any more elephants. That's all we need—to get stomped flat by one of those things!"

The Sleepers journeyed hard for the next three days. The rising plain gave way to low-lying foothills, and the vegetation became more luxuriant. On the fourth day they came to jungle.

Trees towered high over their heads—so high that they cut off the sun at times, and the lack of sunlight had killed off all the vegetation far below. That made walking easier, but after a time this gave way to smaller trees, and the undergrowth became thicker.

Reb eyed the dense growth ahead. "We're going to have to hack our way through this," he said. "Let me go first, and when I give out, Josh, you can take over."

"That sounds good," Josh said. "Stick together, now. I'd hate to get lost in this mess."

Reb walked ahead, slashing at the vines with the razor-keen machete. He worked tirelessly for an hour, then Josh took his place. He lasted almost that long. Dave, who was third, was not as handy with a machete as the other two. He lasted only half an hour. Then Jake said, "Let me at that stuff. I can use either hand, not like you righties or lefties."

Wash said, "Yeah, he's amphibious. He can use either hand."

"An amphibian is an *alligator* or something like that!" Jake said. He waded in manfully, and the little column wound its way through the thick jungle. It was exhausting going, and the bugs swarmed, biting their exposed hands and faces.

Toward sunset, Josh called a halt in plenty of time to build a fire and cook a good meal. They slept like the dead that night.

The next two days were just as hard going. Sometimes they came to wild, fierce rivers that were difficult to ford. They saw many signs of wild animals. Once Reb glimpsed what he thought was a lion, but it slunk away before he could unloose an arrow after it.

The following morning, they had traveled not more than two hours when suddenly Josh said, "Look, that's smoke up there!"

"Either a forest fire," Sarah said, "or maybe a village."

"According to the map," Josh said, "there ought to be a river there and a little village, if we've done our navigating right."

They were all eager to find some kind of civilization.

"I hope they're friendly. I used to read in *National Geographic* about pygmies," Dave said with a worried look. "They had blowguns, and they would shoot you with poison darts."

Abbey moved closer to Dave and did not get far from him as they made their way along a path that showed signs of human use.

The vegetation thinned out, and at last, when they turned a corner, they saw a small huddle of grass huts and several fires going in the middle of the encampment. A number of people were moving around.

Josh said, "Let's not scare them—give them a chance to look us over."

They had not gone much farther before a cry went up, and they were soon ringed by natives. They were brown-skinned people, smaller than the Sleepers, and they spoke a broken form of the common language of Nuworld.

"We are on a mission from Goél," Josh told them, holding his hand up in the sign of peace. He saw at once that the name *Goél* meant something to these people.

The tallest among them—perhaps their leader— was a man of about fifty but with white hair. He grinned, exposing broken teeth. "Goél! We are followers of Goél."

"Great!" Josh said. He explained their mission, and the villagers and the chief listened.

"Come in," the chief invited. "We have feast tonight."

"I could stand somebody else's cooking," Reb said to Wash. "I hope they don't feed us monkey, though."

Truthfully, they half expected to be fed something outlandish. But in fact, they were served fish and wild pig, which had been roasted by turning the whole carcass over a fire.

"Sure wish I had some good barbecue sauce to go with this here pig," Reb said, "but we take it as it comes."

During the feast, the Sleepers were entertained by the natives, who performed a rather strange dance in which they stomped the ground rapidly in unison and clapped their hands together.

"You want to dance, Abbey?" Dave said, chewing on a piece of the roast pork, which was delicious. "You're always one for a dance."

"Not *that* kind of dance," Abbey said.

"Well, you're not likely to get a waltz out of this bunch. Look at them stomp. I'll bet they're all flat-footed."

After the entertainment, the chief made a long speech. He spoke about how Goél had once visited their village and how they had committed themselves to him. "We very glad to see servants of our master, Goél," he said finally. "Now, *you* make speech."

Josh hated to make speeches, but Sarah whispered, "Get up, Josh. Tell them what we're going to do. Make them feel good about following Goél."

Josh stood and began his speech. He quickly learned that these people had somehow heard of the Seven Sleepers, even out in this far reach of the jungle. That surprised him. He had not realized how far the power and the name of Goél had reached.

Nevertheless, he was pleased. He said, "We are on a mission for Goél, and we could use some help. We would like for some of you to escort us, if you would, to the land of Fedor."

A shout went up.

Josh was startled—what had he said? He looked around at the other Sleepers, who appeared to be as mystified as he was. "What's the matter?" he asked the chief, who was shaking his head violently. "What's wrong with Fedor?"

"No go Fedor," the chief said, almost sullenly.

"Why not? What's wrong with it?" Josh said.

"Bad place. Fedor bad place. Hurt our people, steal our people."

This was all that Josh could get out of the chief,

and it seemed that their friendly relations were at an end, at least for the moment.

That night the young men slept in one hut, while the girls were put in another. The boys talked together about the chief's reactions.

Wash said, "Doesn't sound like no place we'd go for a vacation, this here Fedor."

"That chief was plumb scared of them," Reb said thoughtfully. "Wonder what they're like. Couldn't be any worse than some of the critters we already met."

"One thing's clear," Josh put in. "They're not going to take us anywhere. We'll have to make it ourselves."

The villagers were quick to give them fresh food to take with them but evidently were relieved when the Sleepers bade them farewell the next day.

When they were out of sight of the village, Josh said, "Well, no help from them, but at least we're on track." He pulled out the map as they walked along. "I figure we ought to make it in about three more days."

They made a good two-day trip. Then on the afternoon of the third day, they came to a small river.

"I'd like to stop and camp here for the night," Josh said, "but it's too early. We can make another ten miles before sundown."

"Let's just rest a minute," Abbey said, slipping her pack off. "I'm tired."

"And we might as well eat up the last of that meat that them folks gave us back there," Reb said.

Jake started for the river. "I'm just gonna go see how deep this thing is. It looks pretty swift."

He waded out into it, and in the meantime Reb tasted the meat. "*Fah!*" he said. "Spoiled!" He threw it into the water, and the instant the meat hit, it disappeared. There was the rolling flash of a white belly, and Reb yelled, "*Jake, get back here!*"

Jake turned and said, "What?" He looked at Reb waving frantically at the river—which suddenly seemed to be filled with fish, all headed straight for him. He scrambled back to the bank, his face pale and his lips trembling. "What's that *in* there?"

Josh had seen the piece of meat disappear, and now he walked down closer to the water. "Throw another piece in, Reb." He watched as Reb tossed another chunk.

Instantly it disappeared.

"Well," Josh said, "it's a good thing you didn't try to wade out farther, Jake. Those things are meat-eating fish—piranha, maybe."

"I heard those things can strip a cow in a matter of minutes," Reb said. He swallowed hard. "I guess we're going to have to find a bridge to cross this here river."

A little later they came to a large tree that had fallen across the narrow river.

Josh helped Sarah to the other side, saying, "Be careful, now. Couldn't afford to lose you."

Abbey crossed quickly, assisted by Dave, and the rest followed.

Reb threw the rest of his meat into the water, and there was a splashing as it was slashed by keen teeth and devoured. "Well," he said, "that's about the fanciest garbage disposal I ever saw."

Josh appreciated Reb's cheerful courage, but he said, "Let's get away from this. Maybe we can find a river not filled with that kind of fish."

5

Sleepers to the Rescue

Ow!" Jake slapped at his neck where a mosquito had bitten him viciously. Staring at his hand, now smeared with blood, Jake said mournfully, "These mosquitoes are going to eat us alive!"

Reb, walking along behind him, spoke up. "You call these skeeters? Back home in Arkansas around Stuttgart, you'd faint if you'd see what we had there."

"They couldn't have been any worse than these," Jake protested.

"Worse? I'll tell you how bad they were," Reb said. "I got caught out duck huntin' once in the rice fields. The skeeters started coming in about dark, and I run over and got in the car and shut the doors and rolled the windows up. But that didn't stop them. No sirree! Not them skeeters."

Josh, who should have known better, asked, "How'd they get at you inside the car?"

"Why, them skeeters just drilled right through the top of it with them sharp beaks of theirs."

Sarah laughed. "I never heard of skeeters like that. Did they get you?"

"No, I just took my hammer out," Reb said, "and I bradded their bills on the inside of the car—but that didn't work too good either."

Wash, who was grinning broadly, said, "What'd they do then?"

"Why, they just flew off with that car—with me inside it."

"How'd you get out of that one?" Dave was peering ahead into the dense jungle and was only half listening to the conversation.

"I didn't," Reb said. He laughed wildly. "They killed me!"

Reb's stories were entertaining, and the Sleepers needed entertainment. They had been plodding through the jungle until their legs were trembling with fatigue, and the insects plagued them constantly.

Snakes, too, appeared without warning. They had killed several with the machete. Abbey was so frightened of them that all she could do was freeze, shut her eyes, and scream at the top of her lungs.

Josh said, "I don't like this idea of just plunging on. We don't know what's ahead of us."

"I been thinking about that," Reb said. "Why don't you let me go out, and I could be a vedette."

"What's a *vedette?*" Sarah demanded.

"A vedette? Why, shoot, that's an army term. Back in the Civil War they would send out scouts on horseback. They was called vedettes."

"Well, you don't have any horse, but it wouldn't be a bad idea to go out and sort of see what's ahead of us, Reb. You're the best in the woods."

"OK," Reb said cheerfully. "You all just kind of hang back. I'll mosey on ahead and see what's up there."

The young Southerner ran off lightly, despite the heavy pack on his back, and disappeared into the green foliage.

"He is one tough guy," Dave said "It seems like nothing bothers him—sun, mosquitoes, or snakes." He shook his head. "I wish we had about five hundred of him on our side."

"So do I," Josh said. "And it seems he never gets

tired. As lean and lanky as he is, he just doesn't wear out."

The remaining Sleepers pressed on slowly. The jungle here was not as thick as some stretches they had been through, though there were still some tall trees, and howler monkeys appeared from time to time overhead, their mouths wide open, screaming loudly.

Jake paused to look up at one, not twenty feet over his head. The animal's eyes were bulging and his mouth was agape, emitting the most piercing screams.

"Do you know," Jake remarked, "that reminds me of Miss Brown, my ninth-grade algebra teacher." He thought about that for a moment. "She was sure ugly!"

Sarah smiled. "I doubt she was ugly. I think you likely had a bad attitude. No human was ever as ugly as these howler monkeys."

They forged on, fortunately seeing no more snakes. The sun was going down behind the tall trees, and Josh knew they would soon have to camp for the night. He had just started keeping an eye out for a likely campsite when all of a sudden he heard a noise and straightened up quickly. He kept his eyes on the trail ahead and drew a sigh of relief when he saw Reb come running.

Then Josh grew tense, for Reb was not smiling. "What's wrong, Reb?" he called out.

Reb pulled up, his face covered with sweat and his chest heaving. "Got some real trouble up there," he gasped.

"Take it easy, Reb. Catch your breath," Dave said. He waited until Reb regained some breath, then said, "What did you see up there—is it more elephants?"

"It's worse than that. It looks like a Tarzan movie."

"You mean there's a bunch of natives up there?" Abbey said fearfully, looking into the jungle as if she could see through it.

"There's a mess of them, and they're up to no good."

"What did you see?" Josh asked.

"I couldn't believe it at first. There was all these natives, and they's around what looked like a post. Maybe it was a tree they had cut off. Anyhow, they had this young lady tied to it." He paused and shook his head in disbelief at what he had seen. "And what's more, she was a white girl!"

"Out here in the jungle?" Sarah asked. "You must've seen it wrong."

"Nothing wrong with my eyesight," Reb declared. "She was white, and what's more, she had red hair. Even redder than yours, Jake."

Jake blinked. "What's a redheaded white girl doing out in this part of the world?"

"I don't know," Reb said, "but she's not long for this world if I don't mistake it."

"What do you mean?" Josh demanded.

"I mean it looked like they was fixin' to do her in," Reb stated flatly. His eyes narrowed. "They was puttin' some sticks around her feet. I think they're going to burn her up."

"Well, we can't let that happen," Dave said.

Josh thought quickly. "No, we can't. How many were there, Reb?"

"Oh, there must have been at least forty or fifty, I reckon. I didn't stop to count, but we better hurry up, because they're winding up for mischief."

"All right," Josh said, "if we can catch them off guard, I think we can do some good. Everybody get your bows out. We may need them. And put your quivers on your back. Reb," he asked, "can you lead us back there and put us within range without being seen?"

52

"I think I might," Reb said. "They're down in a valley. If we get up along the sides of the cliffs, we ought to be able to fill 'em full of arrows like pincushions, but we better hurry."

Quickly the Sleepers removed their bows and strung them. When they had settled the quivers over their backs, Josh said, "You lead the way. Get us where we should go, and then we'll decide what to do."

"I know," Dave said. He pulled out the alarm that Jake had given him for his birthday. "Why don't I punch this thing? That'd be enough to scare 'em to death, if they're superstitious."

"That's good," Josh agreed quickly. "Now let's go."

Reb jogged off and the others followed. Wash and Abbey were the slowest, bringing up the rear, and Jake stayed back with them to hurry them along.

Finally Reb threw up a hand, signaling them to stop. "Maybe we can get on both sides of this ravine. Let me take Jake and Wash with me, and the rest of you stay on this side. Give us time to get over there, and when it's time, you let that there alarm off."

"All right," Dave said.

Reb suddenly looked at Josh. His eyes narrowed. "What about it, Josh? Do we shoot to kill?"

It was a bad moment for Josh Adams. He was by nature a gentle boy, but he had seen much death. Now it was hard for him to face Reb and the others. They all stood waiting. He thought, *If we don't go all out, there's so many of them they'll kill that girl and then get us as well.*

Slowly he nodded. "Scare them off if we can. Self-defense if we have to. I hate to do it, but it may be necessary in order to rescue her. In that case, take the best shots you can and shoot quick. Make those arrows really rain down—it's the only chance we've got."

"All right, you've got it," Reb said.

Josh said, "Sarah, you and Abbey come along with Dave and me. Be quiet now."

Josh's heart was pounding as he crept toward the edge of the cliff. Fortunately it was covered with brush and large trees, which hid them.

Now as the Sleepers spread out along both sides of the ravine, he could hear the sound of a drum beating. Branches scratched his face, and he kept his bow protected. Finally, he came to where the brush parted, so that he could see what was happening in the valley below.

Josh took a deep breath, for he saw a young girl tied to a tree that had been lopped off at the top. Her skin was indeed fair, and her hair was, as Reb had said, red. She appeared to be in her late teens, and he noticed that she was very attractive. She was wearing a skirt made out of some kind of animal hide, and a gold metallic halter protected her upper body. She wore a belt with a shiny buckle, and altogether she made a pathetic picture as she stood there at the mercy of the savages.

Dave said, "She's sure not a Nuworlder like any we've seen. But look at those warriors—they look like something out of a comic book."

Josh nodded. "They look pretty rough, all right." He was eyeing the men. They had tattoos in hideous patterns all over their faces. That made them look even fiercer than they probably were. All carried spears and oddly shaped knives in their belts, and they raised the spears now, chanting in a language that none of the Sleepers understood.

"We'd better hurry and do something," Abbey said.

"See, they're getting ready to light that fire. They're going to burn her alive!"

"We can't wait any longer," Josh said. "Notch your arrows." He slipped the arrow on his own bow and pulled the string to test the tension. He picked his target—one of the larger men, who held a torch, ready to light the fire. Another man, who could have been the chief, stood off to one side. His face was tattooed with blue and red figures, and he had a mouth like a shark's. "Get ready with the signal, Dave. Then try to hit the chief there, if you have to. I'll get the guy with the torch."

"Just look at that girl," Sarah said. "She's got plenty of courage."

Josh saw that was true. The young woman had thrown her head back and was laughing at her captors, taunting them in their own language.

Abruptly the chief cried out a command, and the torchbearer advanced.

Josh pulled the arrow back to his ear, and almost instantly the hideous squawk of Jake's siren split the air.

The native with the torch froze. Arrows zipped into the trees. One grazed the chief's headdress. He called commands, but the warriors cried out in fear over the howl of the siren and what they probably thought was an attack. The chief shouted another command, and the natives retreated.

Suddenly a familiar cry rent the air, and Sarah said, "That's Reb giving the Rebel yell. I think we won. Let's go down and help that girl."

"But keep your arrows ready," Josh warned. "They might come back."

"I don't think so," Dave said. "They took off like every piranha in the river was after them."

The four Sleepers scrambled down the embankment, and Josh saw Reb coming down from the other side with Wash and Jake. He called, "Reb, keep an eye out. Some of those birds might come back."

"Right," Reb said, "but I don't think so."

All of them kept their eyes on the spot where the natives had disappeared. But they were equally curious about the strange girl.

Josh saw that she was studying him calmly. "Hello," he said, "are you all right?" He was not certain if the girl would understand the common language of Nuworld, but apparently she did, for she nodded.

"Yes. Where did you come from, and who are you?" she asked.

"Well, you're a pretty cool customer," Reb said. He stepped behind the tree, pulled out his knife, and cut the thongs that bound her.

Rubbing her wrists to restore circulation, the girl looked around at them curiously. She did not seem to have any fear at all.

Sarah said, "Did they hurt you?"

"No," the young woman said coolly. She was a tall girl and well proportioned. Her arms were strongly developed, and obviously she was a runner, for her legs were well muscled. All in all she was a healthy-looking specimen, and she had light green eyes that gave her almost an oriental look because they were almond shaped. "Who are you?" she asked again.

"I'm Josh Adams, and this is Sarah—" He named all the Sleepers and then said, "I'm glad we got here in time. I think they were about ready to kill you, weren't they?"

"They are our enemies, the Londo tribe. That was Ulla, their chief. They captured me early this morning while I was out hunting."

"What's your name?" Sarah asked.

"I am Princess Merle."

"Another princess?" Jake said. He had met several before, and he caught Sarah's warning as she cleared her throat.

"Well, Princess, I'm glad we got here in time." Josh could not help asking, "Weren't you a little bit afraid when they were about to touch that fire off?"

"The daughters of Fedor are not afraid to die," Merle said calmly. "But who *are* you? I've never seen people like you before. Where do you come from?"

"We come from far away, and we are looking for the village of Fedor."

Princess Merle examined him, apparently considering his words.

She had an attractive face, he thought, with well-shaped lips and high cheekbones. Her hair hung down her back, and she had tied it with a single band of what seemed to be gold.

"Why do you seek the people of Fedor?"

"We're sent by our master, Goél," Josh said. "We come in peace to talk to your chief."

"You come in peace?" Merle asked suspiciously. "We do not have peaceful relations with other peoples."

"I think we proved we want to be friends," Dave said. He stepped forward to look down at the princess from his greater height. "We wouldn't have saved your life if we didn't come in a peaceable manner."

Merle stared at Dave with great interest. She had to tilt back her head to look up, for he was wearing boots that added to his height. "Are all the men as tall as you in your country?"

Dave blinked with surprise. "Some of them are. Reb there's taller than I am." He waited until Merle had inspected Reb and then turned her eyes back to him. "Why do you ask?"

"Our men are not so tall," Merle said. There was a speculative light in her eyes, and she turned her head to one side, studying all the Sleepers. She put her gaze on Abbey. "What is that on your face?" she asked.

"Why—it's makeup."

"Makeup? What is that?" Merle stepped up and touched Abbey's lips, then looked at the red mark on her finger. "Your mouth is bleeding."

"That's lipstick," Abbey said.

Merle studied her, then turned to Sarah. "Are you the leader?" she asked. "You are the biggest."

"Why, no. Josh here is the leader."

Surprise caused the girl's eyes to fly open. She turned back to look at Josh. "That is unusual."

Josh thought that she meant that Dave would make a better leader, and he said stiffly, "Goél selects who will be the leaders among us." Then he said, "But can you take us to your village? We need to talk to your chief."

"I can do that," the girl said. "We must go before dark. Travel then would be dangerous. The tiger roams after dark, and even you would not be able to defeat him."

Reb was insulted. "I never saw a tiger I was afraid of."

"Is that right? Then you never saw the tigers around here." Merle smiled. The smile made her look younger, and she laughed a surprisingly light laugh. "Come then, I will take you to my village."

The young woman covered the ground at a swift pace.

As the Sleepers followed her, Abbey said, "She's a

brazen hussy, isn't she? I never saw a girl like her before."

"She's very brave," Sarah answered. "But I wonder why she thought I was the leader."

Abbey did not answer. It took all her breath just to keep up with the group. Night was falling fast, and the mention of tigers did not make staying outside the village enticing. Abbey put herself in the middle of the line, for it made her feel safer. She knew that none of them felt safe, for somewhere Ulla, chief of the Londos, was out there looking for revenge.

6

Another Fine Mess

A first-time journey always seems far, Josh thought. *When we're familiar with the distance, the traveling time seems to shrink.*

As the Sleepers followed Princess Merle along trails that twisted through forest, over hills, and across brown streams of water, he whispered to Sarah, "I wish we'd get there. It seems like this goes on forever."

"So do I. It's getting dark, and I've been thinking about those tigers. Why is it that a tiger seems so much worse than a lion?"

"Well, they're bigger, for one thing," Jake said. "A lion won't weigh over two hundred pounds or two fifty, but a tiger can weigh four hundred or even more. Just one snap, and you're gone with those dudes."

Sarah gave a shudder and moved closer to Josh, her arm brushing his. "I can't get over how strange that princess is. She seems to have no nerves at all. If they'd been about to light a fire under *my* feet, I think I would have screamed loud enough to wake the dead."

"Me too." Jake seemed unable to restrain a slight shudder himself. "Can't think of many things worse than getting burned to death while you're alive."

He had no sooner said this than the princess called back, "I see we cannot make it back to my village tonight. We must take shelter before the tiger comes."

"That suits me fine," Dave said, "but how are you going to hide from a tiger? They can climb trees, can't they?"

"Yes, they can, but there is a safe place. I've used it often."

The Sleepers followed as the princess led them off the main pathway and to the sheer face of a cliff. She pointed upward. "There! There's a cave, you see. Come this way."

Along with the others, Reb scrambled after the young woman, panting. "She must be half mountain goat. I never did like high places."

Wash grunted. "I like it better than being tiger bait." He was sure-footed, and although the path cut out of the mountainside was narrow, that didn't seem to trouble him. "Don't fall off, Reb. You'd bust your head, sure enough—*and don't look down.*"

Josh entered the cavern directly behind the princess, then helped Sarah and Abbey through the opening. After that he looked around and was surprised to see that it was a good-sized cave. The ceiling at the entrance was at least eight feet high, and it sloped backward some twenty feet.

Behind him, Reb drew a sigh of relief as he came to the opening and stumbled inside. "Well, I'm up, but I don't know if I'll ever get down."

"This cave looks man-made," Josh said. "How did it get here?"

"It was cut a long time ago," Merle said, "probably as a place to hide from the tiger or other enemies. There's wood over there. We can have a fire."

"Good. We've got a little food left, and I wouldn't mind having some," Reb said. He supervised the fire building, and soon the smell of frying meat filled the cave.

Merle watched curiously, sitting with her back against the wall. Her green eyes glittered as the firelight reflected off them. Abruptly she asked Sarah, "You cook?"

"Why, of course," Sarah said. "Don't you?"

"No."

The answer was so terse that Abbey and Sarah stared at each other. Abbey said curiously, "I thought all girls do something about cooking."

"No, I do not cook."

"Is it because you're a princess?" Dave asked. He was sitting across from Merle, staring at the bands that were on her upper arm. They looked as if they were made of gold, and they shone faintly in the half darkness.

"No, the daughters of Fedor do not cook."

"Must get pretty hungry," Reb said. He grinned at Sarah and Abbey. "I hope *you* don't take it into your heads to quit cooking. I'd hate to have to eat my own."

Sarah said, "I'd hate to have to eat your own too. I've tried to eat your cooking before, Reb. Here, this piece is almost done."

Abbey served the meat on the small plates they carried with them. There was no extra plate, so Josh put some meat on his and handed it to the princess. "I hope you like this. It's deer of some kind. We shot it yesterday."

Merle nodded when she had tasted it. "Yes, it is timbok. Very good—young and tender. How long was your shot?"

"Oh, about fifty yards, I guess."

"That is a good shot. I'm surprised that you're so good. Are you the best with a bow?" She looked at Sarah and asked, "Is he better than you?"

Actually Sarah was better than Josh. But then, she was better than any of the other Sleepers and did not like to brag.

Josh didn't mind telling, however. "She's the best shot of all of us."

His answer seemed to please Princess Merle. She nodded slightly. "That is as it should be."

Her response puzzled him.

She began asking questions then about the place they came from. They finished their meal, taking turns telling her about some of their adventures. She drank from Dave's canteen and examined it carefully. "This is good—better than animal skin," she said.

"I guess it is," Dave said. "We may have an extra one for a gift for the chief."

"It will be welcome," Princess Merle said. She looked around again and asked, "Why are you different colors, and why are some of you bigger than others?"

"Well, I guess we all come from different places, and we're not related to each other—just good friends. We've come from all over Oldworld."

"Oldworld?"

"Well . . . yes." Josh launched into a long explanation of how they came to be in Nuworld. He saw that the concept was entirely foreign to the princess. Finally he asked, "Have you ever heard of Goél?"

"No, who is Goél? Is he a warrior?"

"Well, I think he might be if he set his mind to it." Josh smiled. "I thought you might have heard of him."

"No. Have you ever heard of Maug?"

"Maug?" The name had an ugly sound, and Josh shook his head. "No, who is he?"

"We serve Maug, we of the Fedor people. He is strong."

Instantly Josh caught Sarah's eye. They knew at once that she was talking about some sort of god. It did not seem the right time to talk about such things, so he said simply, "Well, we'll talk about that when we meet your chief. What's your father's name?"

An odd light came into her eyes. "His name is Chava."

"Chief Chava—well, I'll be glad to meet him," Dave said, smiling at her. "But right now I think we'd better get some sleep."

Most of them were tired, and they rolled up in their blankets. Sarah brought out the one extra blanket they carried and said, "Here, Princess, you can wrap up in this for the night."

"The daughters of Fedor do not need such things," Merle said. Nevertheless she took the blanket and felt it curiously. "What's it made out of?"

"It's wool," Sarah said. "Do you have sheep here?"

"What is sheep?"

Merle listened with apparent interest while Sarah explained the process of extracting wool and making garments from it. Then she said, "No, we wear animal hides like this." She touched her skirt, which was made of very soft, fine leather.

"Wool is much warmer," Abbey said. "More comfortable too, I'd think."

"Our women do not seek comfort but glory."

It was a strange statement, and for a moment there was silence. All of the Sleepers had heard the remark, but there was no comment. Finally Sarah said, "Well, you can have the glory. I'll take a nice warm blanket. Good night."

"Good night," Princess Merle said. She sat with her back against the cave wall, facing the fire and holding the blanket.

Her eyes were half hooded as she stared into the dying blaze, and Josh, watching her, thought, *What a strange girl!*

The next morning they ate a quick breakfast. Afterward, Merle seemed interested mostly in Abbey, who insisted on putting on a little makeup. It amused the red-haired girl, and she said, "Why do you do that?"

"That's a good question." Dave grinned. "I'd like to hear the answer to that myself."

"I can tell you," Jake said. "To make herself attractive to the guys."

"What is a 'guy'?"

"Oh, I mean men. That's what lipstick and powder and all that stuff is for."

"It's just to make you look better!" Abbey insisted, though she flushed. "Would you like to try some, Princess?"

Princess Merle stared at her with amusement in her eyes. "I do not think so. Our women do not care to make themselves attractive to men."

"Then they're different from any women I ever heard of," Dave said. He got to his feet and stretched, touching the ceiling easily. "I'm glad you knew about this place," he said to the princess.

They left the cave then and made their descent. As they walked along, the jungle grew less dense. Merle, Josh noticed, kept her eyes constantly on the move—perhaps watching for enemies, possibly for game.

Dave said, "Tell us a little bit about your people."

"We are a strong people, and courage is the most valuable thing in our opinion. The one who has the most courage is the one we admire the most."

"Well, courage is a fine thing. Among us, I guess Reb there probably has more of that in him than anybody else. If he's afraid of anything, nobody ever found out about it."

"What about Sarah and Abbey?"

"Well, what about them?" Dave sounded confused.

"Do they have the most courage?"

Dave seemed puzzled by the turn the conversation had taken. "I suppose they have as much courage as any girl could have."

His answer brought Princess Merle's head around, and she studied him. Then she asked more questions about the Sleepers. She seemed fascinated by them. She also spoke often of Maug.

Finally Josh asked, "Who exactly is this Maug?"

"He is the god of Fedor. When we are strong, he helps us. He gives us courage, but he is a demanding god."

Josh thought about that, and then a suspicion came to him. "Those folks that were about to burn you—do they serve Maug too?"

"They are nothing," Princess Merle said.

"Were they sacrificing you to *their* god?"

"Of course. Why else would they do it?"

Josh didn't answer for a moment. Then he said, "Would you sacrifice one of *them* to Maug?"

"Why, yes!" Surprise was in her voice, and the loveliness of her eyes was in contrast with the cold-blooded way she had answered his question. "Do you not sacrifice your enemies to your Goél?"

"No, Goél's not like that. He doesn't demand vengeance or anything like that. As a matter of fact, he has concern for every person."

"He must be a weak god then."

Josh knew something was wrong with the way this conversation was going. He was starting to say more when suddenly Reb yelled, *"Look out!"*

The Seven Sleepers made wild grabs for their swords, but then Josh called out, "Hold it! Don't pull your weapons."

"I don't reckon it'd do any good anyway," Reb said.

67

From almost nowhere the Sleepers and Merle had been surrounded. They stood facing a sea of spears and gleaming short swords.

"Look at that!" Jake said. "I never saw the like of it."

"Me either," Wash said. "Who *are* these people?"

The newcomers surrounding them were obviously from Fedor. All were women. Most of them had fair skin and light hair. All were dressed in clothes identical to what Princess Merle wore.

Josh was uneasy, for he saw that these women meant business. There was a cruel glitter in their eyes, and he was sure it was only Merle who saved them by saying, "Stop! Do not kill them."

"Amazons. That's what they look like," Sarah murmured. "Amazon women."

Josh instantly thought of the legendary breed of women he had read about. They had been women warriors, who wore armor and carried weapons and were fierce in battle. Swallowing hard, he looked around and said, "I always thought they were just in storybooks, but it looks like we found the book."

7
Male and Female

The Amazon-like women who surrounded the Sleepers herded them along. Their weapons had been stripped from them immediately, and if they lagged they were prodded forward at sword point.

Josh tried to speak to Princess Merle. He suggested that there was some ingratitude involved here—after all, they had saved her life! "You don't have to take us prisoners like this," he protested.

Princess Merle strode along in front of the captives. She had been given a sword, which she now wore belted around her trim waist. The glance she gave him was cool and calculating. She did not even answer him but said, "Sarah, you and Abbey come up here. Let the men go last."

Abbey shot a quick glance at Sarah as the two were hurried forward. "What does it all mean?" she whispered.

"I think it's a male-female thing," Sarah whispered. She had quickly grasped that the women warriors had little respect for the guys, although they did look with speculation at the tall forms of Reb, Josh, and Dave. Since poor Jake and Wash were smaller, they were treated rather roughly, being struck by the flat of the sword several times.

The procession made its way for half an hour, and the trail grew broader all the time. Finally, it opened up onto a rather attractive village of houses made of upright wooden stakes and having cone-shaped thatched roofs. A stake stockade was built around the village, its top sharpened to needlelike points.

The gates swung open on some sort of hinges, and as soon as the troop was inside, they closed at once with a kind of grim finality.

"I don't like this, Dave," Josh muttered. "It looks like we're not going to get a very good reception."

Dave was looking at the women with narrowed eyes. "They sure do look like Amazons," he said, "or at least what I thought Amazons might look like. But where are the men?"

As the Sleepers looked around, they discovered that some men were there, but all were unarmed and looked harmless. As a matter of fact, they looked almost cowed, and they were generally smaller than the women.

"These are sure funny people," Wash said. He'd just been given a blow with the flat of a sword. "I never saw such mean-looking ladies in all my life! They look like they'd be wrestlers if they were back in Oldworld."

"They do look pretty bad," Jake agreed. "And the men—there's something wrong with them. Look how they kind of sneak around."

Josh had no time to examine the crowd further, for they had come into an open space where a platform was built about two feet off the ground.

On it sat a woman in a chair made of carved, dark wood. She was blonde like the others, with blue eyes, and was obviously tall. She wore a headdress composed of feathers with some sort of green stones on the band. Josh realized at once that she was not young. There were scars on her arms, and her right leg was twisted, as though she'd been injured at one time. He decided this was no one important.

He thought, *Where's the chief? What did she say his name was?*

Immediately, however, he was set straight, for Princess Merle went right up onto the platform and bowed to the woman. "Queen Mother," she said, "these strangers I found on our land."

She turned then to the Sleepers. "This is Queen Faya, warrior queen of the daughters of Fedor."

Josh had to make an instant reevaluation. Obviously Chava, Merle's father, was of little influence. Was he the man standing over to the queen's left? He was short and had reddish hair like Merle's. He said nothing, but his eyes moved to the queen as though he waited to hear what she would say.

"What are you doing on our land?" Queen Faya demanded. She had a strong voice, and Josh got the impression that she hated being bound to her chair. She had obviously been a strong woman in her youth—and would have to be, he thought, to head these fierce women who made up the fighting arm of the Fedor tribe.

Josh announced his name and said, "We come on behalf of our sire, Goél."

"I know no one named Goél."

"He is the mighty leader who is going to deliver Nuworld from its bondage," Josh said. "The powers of darkness will spread no more when Goél and his house crush the Dark Lord."

At mention of the words *Dark Lord*, a strange figure suddenly emerged. She was a woman of some sixty or perhaps seventy years, with gray hair and sharp black eyes. She was wearing all sorts of what looked to be jewelry—brass plates with enigmatic markings on them. Her headdress was red and yellow feathers, and the necklace of bone around her neck jangled as she hopped before the queen.

"These men are the enemies of Maug!" she screamed. "We know no one named Goél. Do not trust them, my Queen!"

"I do not trust them," Queen Faya said. She stared at the Sleepers, and then her eyes went to her daughter. "How did you find them?"

"I had been captured by Ulla and his band. They were about to sacrifice me to their god when these came to my rescue."

At least, Josh thought, *she told the truth.* He was, however, disappointed when Merle made little of the rescue.

"They came here with me, and now they are, of course, our captives."

"Wait a minute," Josh said, "we came on a peaceful mission. After all, we did save your daughter's life."

Queen Faya did not seem impressed. Her blue eyes were cold as polar ice as she studied Josh almost clinically.

Then a man stepped forward and spoke up. "My Queen," he said, "these people are not our enemies."

"Zuriel, you are a historian, but *I* will make the decision about captives," Queen Faya said. Her words fell like blows on the man, and he retreated silently into the crowd.

"I will claim that tall one for my own."

The Sleepers turned their heads to see a big woman step out from the throng. She came to stand before the throne. "Sister, I call the blood kin and claim this captive." She pointed at Dave with an air of possession.

Queen Faya's lips turned upward in a rather grim smile. "You are thinking of Ettore, Marden?"

"Perhaps I am. This one is tall and strong, and we need good blood in our line." She made a motion, and

72

a girl of nineteen or twenty came forward. She had dark hair and black eyes, in contrast to most of the women warriors, who were fair. Her eyes glittered as she walked up to Dave, who watched her cautiously. Carelessly she reached out and felt the muscles of his arm, then commanded, "Let me see your teeth."

Dave, outraged, shook off her grasp. "I'm not showing my teeth to anyone!"

Immediately the girl slapped him, hard. The blow drove him backwards, and the print of her hand was on his face in white.

"Keep your mouth shut, or I will shut it for you," the girl Ettore said. She turned and nodded. "I will take this one, my Mother."

"I will decide who will receive the captives!" Princess Merle said. "I captured them. The decision will be mine."

Again Faya smiled as she looked at her daughter. "And which do *you* choose, daughter?"

"*I* will take the tall one. He is strong and might make a good mate. Come here!" she commanded Dave.

Dave started to protest, but Josh said hastily, "Better do as she says, Dave. We can straighten it all out later."

"All right, then." Dave moved over to stand by her side.

Then Merle said, "I will have the young female also." She pointed to Abbey. "I do not think she will ever make a warrior."

Marden cried out again. "Sister Queen, I claim the right of blood. Give me a choice."

"Very well." The queen seemed already tired of the scene.

Marden, with a look of triumph, said, "I will take this one." She pointed to Josh.

Her daughter said, "And we will take the tall female. She might make a warrior maid if we toughen her up some."

Sarah stayed close to Josh as they walked to where Marden and Ettore stood.

Queen Faya said, "Who else chooses one of these?"

"I do. I want the tall one with the light hair."

Reb blinked as another woman came forward. She was not lean and strong like the others. Because she stood with the trim, tanned women warriors, she seemed somewhat overweight. She was rather pretty, though, with large blue eyes, a round face, and a crop of yellow hair. She came up to Reb and touched his hair. "I will have this one, and I will take the little one too." She motioned toward Wash.

"Let it be so then," Queen Faya said. "We will hear their stories later."

Reb's owner seemed delighted with her acquisition. She grabbed his arm, saying, "Come with me."

She dragged him off, and Wash followed helplessly.

Reb looked back over his shoulder. "I don't like this, Josh."

"I don't like it either, Reb. We'll see how it goes."

"You will come now." The warrior maiden named Ettore grabbed Josh's hair and gave it a vicious pull. He did not cry out, and she grinned. "Good. You'll know what to expect if you are disobedient." Then she studied Sarah. "Can you fight?" she demanded bluntly.

Sarah pulled herself up to her full height. She was not as tall as Ettore, but she seemed determined not to show fear. Defiantly she said, "I have fought before."

"Have you ever killed any of your enemies?"

"Yes, I've had to, but I'm not proud of it."

"You will learn better here. If you are to become a warrior maid of the Fedor, you will learn to be proud when you defeat your enemies. Now we go home."

Dave and Abbey were left standing in front of Princess Merle. She watched them, seeming amused by their plight. "I haven't had such fun as this in a long time. Come along, I'll show you your places." She turned to her mother and bowed low. "Queen Mother, I will care for these two captives."

"See that you do."

As the redheaded warrior maid led them away, Abbey felt fear rising in her throat. She knew she could never become one of these women. There was a wildness and a wickedness in their eyes that frightened her, and she stayed as close to Dave as she could as they made their way out of the clearing, headed toward the biggest house in the village.

8

Dave Gets an Education

There was no question of calling Chava "King." Obviously his position in the house was more that of a servant than king or even husband.

Dave noticed that he did show great tenderness and care in helping his wife into the house. Queen Faya could walk using one crutch, but her steps were painful. He watched Chava help her into a chair, put her leg up on a low stool, and bring her something cool to drink.

"He takes care of her like he was her nurse," Abbey whispered.

"I guess that's about what he is."

"Dave, I don't like all this," Abbey said. "Those women, they make me nervous. They're not—they're not normal."

"They sure aren't," Dave said. "A pretty cold-blooded crew, and we've seen some in our time, haven't we?" He saw that she was very frightened and put a hand on her shoulder. "Don't worry. We've gotten out of tougher spots than this. Goél won't let us down." He smiled at her and was glad to see that his assurance seemed to help.

Then a sharp voice said, "Come along, Dave. I'll show you where to sleep. You wait here, Abbey. I want to talk to you alone."

The house was simply built, though it did contain several rooms. One of these was very small, containing only a bunk and a little table, but it had a window that let in the breeze.

When Dave looked down at the bed, he shook his head. "That's pretty short for me."

"So it is," Merle said. "You're very tall. Are all the men where you come from as tall as—" Then she broke off and shook her head. "No, I asked that—and I saw the two smaller ones. Our men are not as tall or as strong as you."

"What's actually going to happen here, Princess? I mean, what am I going to do?"

"Oh, you'll do as you're told. There's plenty of work to be done in a place like this. You may wind up a slave. On the other hand, one of the women may choose you for a mate."

"Where I come from, the men do the choosing."

"You're not where you came from. The quicker you learn that the better." Merle's eyes narrowed. "Let me give you some advice. Keep your mouth shut, do as you're told, and you won't come to any harm, but we have ways of dealing with slaves who don't know their place."

"I'm not a slave!"

"You're not anything until I say so. Remember that. Now, go to sleep. You'll have a long day tomorrow."

Dave waited until she left the room, then went to the door and called after her, "What about something to eat?"

"Tomorrow. There's water in that pot on the table."

Dave was hungry, but there was no arguing. His pack had been taken from him, so what little food he had was lost.

He went to the window and saw that it was not barred. For a moment he thought about escape, but escape to where? They were a hundred miles from the coast. And besides, he knew he couldn't leave his friends.

Discouraged, he walked back to the bed. It was built into the wall, so had only two legs, but it seemed sturdy. A thin pad was on it—cloth stuffed with leaves, he thought. He lay down on it, banged his head on the hard surface underneath, and wished he had a blanket.

There did not seem to be many insects in the air, and he was glad for that. For a long time he lay listening to the sounds outside—and some inside—the house. Finally he went to sleep, thinking, *I can't put up with this forever!*

Dave woke abruptly the next morning, feeling a touch on his shoulder. He started and jumped up, putting a hand out defensively.

"It's only me." Chava smiled at him in a friendly fashion. "Time to fix breakfast. Come, I will show you."

Dave rolled off the bunk and followed the short man into the room that served as kitchen. "Do you cook at all?" Chava asked.

"A little bit," Dave said. "I mean, I don't know what you eat around here."

"It's very simple, really." Chava began to show him how to prepare the meal. Expertly he made cakes out of some sort of ground grain, adding ingredients quickly, and put them in a stone oven, where a fire crackled cheerfully. "Can you milk cattle?"

"Yes, I can do that." Dave nodded. "I'm not very good at it, though."

"We will get the milk." As Chava led the boy out of the hut, Dave looked around but saw no sign of the women.

"Where is everyone?" he asked curiously.

"The women do not arise until we have the breakfast ready."

This did not sit well with Dave, but he realized it was no time to debate the issue. "Do you have other children besides Princess Merle?"

"Yes, a son, Rolf. He is about your own age. You will see him later in the day."

Cautiously Dave began to question Chava and received straightforward answers. It seemed the men took care of the house, milked the cows, did the cooking and the washing and the cleaning.

"What do the women do?" he asked at last.

"Why, they fight, and they hunt."

Dave realized suddenly that not only did the women of Fedor look like Amazons, but the whole culture was based on that concept. Everything was reversed from what he was accustomed to.

This will take some getting used to, and I hope it doesn't last long, he thought. But deep inside he knew this was too far out for him!

For the next two days Dave went through the most humiliating transformation possible. He spent a great deal of time with Chava, learning how to run the details of the house. These were chores that he had never particularly disliked, but that was when the choice had been his. Now each day Princess Merle came in and gave him a particularly hateful cock of her eyebrow and set forth his duties. It was all he could do to keep from from throwing the dishwater in her face.

"Don't mind it, my boy," Chava said kindly. The two of them were peeling potatoes in the kitchen, and Chava had been reminiscing about his own past. He said little about the situation concerning men and women in Fedor but listened as Dave explained how things had been in Oldworld.

Now as the man carefully made a single, long peeling, it dropped into a bucket at his feet. He held up the white potato. "Now, there's a good potato," he said. "I grow these myself. Not everyone can grow potatoes like this."

Dave looked down at his own potatoes and saw that the peelings were thick and that he had wasted much. "I'll never get used to this," he grumbled. "It's not what I was brought up to do." He glared at the door as if he expected Merle to come through it. "You have a beautiful daughter, but I can't stand her."

To Dave's amazement, Chava laughed out loud. "I'm not surprised," he said. "The captives we get from other tribes where men are the superior beings all feel the same way."

"Doesn't it *bother* you?" Dave cried with exasperation. He threw down his potato, picked up another, and began hacking at it. "I mean, after all, you're the *king* of Fedor."

"No, I'm not. I'm the husband of the queen. There's quite a big difference. We have no kings here—only queens. Always."

Dave stopped peeling potatoes, and his brow wrinkled. "I remember something in English history back in Oldworld. Queen Victoria married a man named Albert, and he was *Prince* Albert all his life. Even though he married a queen, he never became a king."

"Was he miserable with that?"

Surprise touched Dave's eyes, and he shook his head slowly. "No, as a matter of fact, they had a very happy life together. Queen Victoria loved him with all her heart, and when he died she wore black for the rest of her life as a sign of mourning."

"I can understand that," Chava said. He peeled his potato slowly, thinking. Then he said, "I love Faya very much, and I believe she loves me."

"Then why does she treat you like a—like a slave?"

"It is the custom," Chava said with surprise. "I suppose I'm used to it. And I like to garden. I like to keep this house. It takes a lot of intelligence, believe it or not. Houses don't just run themselves, and actually, my boy, I could never go out and face a tiger as my wife did."

This caught Dave's attention. "You mean she actually fought a tiger?"

"You probably noticed that her leg is withered. It was mauled by a tiger. She killed him, and that's his pelt she wears as her royal robe, but she's never been the same since." Chava paused. "After all, that's the problem, if your whole life is based on some physical activity. When you get older, you'll either get weaker naturally through age—or perhaps injury will strike you down. Then what do you fall back on?"

Dave frowned. "I saw that happen to some athletes in Oldworld. When they were young and strong, the whole world bowed down to them. But when they got older, they couldn't perform anymore."

"And they were probably very unhappy. But if you think of people who work with their minds—teachers, poets, musicians—they probably had much happier, much more productive lives."

Dave shook his head stubbornly. "That may be so, but I could never be happy living like—well, like you do, Chava."

"No, I think you could not, because it's been born and bred in your bones that men are the strong ones and should rule over the weaker women."

"Well, it's true," Dave said. "I don't think your women *are* strong physically. Why, there's not a one of them that could stand up against me or Reb or Josh with a sword. I'd be willing to test it."

"You'll never get the chance," Chava said. "The warrior maids are a fighting unit. Each one of them is brave and strong and able, but if they see one of their number being overcome, they swarm to her defense."

"I see," Dave said slowly.

He was about to say something else when Princess Merle came through the door. She was wearing an outfit he had not seen before, a skirt made from the pelt of an animal, perhaps a black panther, and an upper garment made of some sort of woven material. He could not help admiring her and thought, *Back in Oldworld she'd make a million bucks a year as a model for one of those fashion houses. But if she didn't like somebody, she'd whack their head off, I suppose.*

"Come with me, Dave," Merle said. She did smile at Chava and say, "I'll have to borrow your helper for a while, Father."

"Of course." He gave the pair a look as they walked out, and muttered, "There's going to be trouble with that pair. Both of them are strong-willed."

"Where are we going?" Dave asked.

"I've got a job for you."

"Look, Merle—"

"Call me Princess," the girl said. "Remember your place."

"All right." Dave shrugged impatiently. "Princess Merle, then. I can't put up with this a whole lot longer. If you want me to do something for you, give me a sword or a bow. You know I'm able to fight beside any one of your women."

"We don't have men fighting beside us. That's not the way things are." There was a shortness in her voice, and she gave him a hard stare. "Don't try to change things, Dave. No matter what they were like back in your world, you're in our world now." Then her voice softened, and she said, "Who knows? You may get chosen by one of the warrior maids as a mate."

Dave yearned to say, "Take all your warrior maids and shove them in a black hole in the sky!" but some wisdom warned him not to provoke her. "What's the job you have in mind?"

"I'll show you." There was a strange smile on her lips, and Dave had learned to hate that.

She led him to one of the outer quarters where they found Abbey standing by a warrior, being instructed in the use of the short sword. Abbey had never been particularly good with weapons, and Dave saw at once that it was a hopeless case.

"Why don't you let *me* do a bout with your warrior maid?" he suggested.

"You have your work to do. Take Abbey's clothes over to those pots and wash them. Be sure you get them clean."

Anger raced through Dave. He glared at Abbey. "Did you ask for me to be your servant?"

"No," Abbey said quickly, "I never said a word."

"*I'm* saying the word. Take those clothes and get going."

"I won't do it!" Dave said. He folded his arms and stared at Princess Merle. "Do what you please—I'm not going to be her servant."

Merle nodded to the warrior who had been teaching Abbey. She drew her own sword, and the two women began to close in on Dave. "Try not to scar him any more than you have to, Freya, but he's got to be taught to mind."

"No, don't hurt him!" Abbey jumped in front of Dave. "Please let me talk to him." Without waiting for an answer, she turned to him and whispered, "Don't mind it. I know it's something you'd rather not do, but we're all doing things we don't want to do." When he still hesitated, she murmured, "Please don't make trouble. You've got to keep yourself whole and unwounded."

Suddenly this made sense to Dave, who, in his blind anger, had forgotten that he had a responsibility to the group. Swallowing hard, he looked over Abbey's head and met the triumphant eyes of Princess Merle and the warrior maiden.

"All right," he said, "I'll do it." Stooping, he grabbed up the clothes in his arms and walked away toward the laundry pots.

A group of men was washing clothes in boiling water, and he joined them.

"I've never seen you before." The speaker was a strong young man, at least five ten, which was about as tall as the men of Fedor ever got. He had muscular shoulders, dark auburn hair bound up with a leather thong, and a pair of strangely colored hazel eyes. He didn't look like any of the Fedorians that Dave had seen. And a spirit of rebellion seemed to leap out of the unusual yellow-brown eyes. "What are you doing here? Where did you come from?"

"From a long way off," Dave said. He began to stir Abbey's clothes with a stick, casting a curious glance at the man. "My name is Dave. You don't look like you belong here either."

"I don't. I'm a captive. My name is Gaelan. When did they take you?"

"Just a few days ago. Have you been here long?"

"Over a month. I swore I'd never be taken alive. But I got knocked in the head somehow, and they brought me here. When I awoke, I was tied up. No choice. I won't stay, though."

Dave looked at the high fence with its sharp stakes and at the guards constantly monitoring it. "Does anybody ever get away—escape, I mean?"

"Not that I know of, but there's always a first." He looked at Dave and said, "You look like a pretty tough fellow—maybe you'll go with me? Two might have more of a chance."

"Maybe I will. I can't stand this place much longer. Where I come from, men are the stronger ones."

"That's the way it is with my people. But I belong to *her* now, or so she says." Gaelan nodded toward Princess Merle. "She's tried to break me, but she hasn't." He grinned, his white teeth gleaming against his tanned face. "I like it when she tries. She can't have her way with *me* anyhow, and that makes her angry."

Merle saw them talking and came over at once. "You don't have enough work to do, Gaelan? Maybe I can find something else."

"Of course, Princess. I can handle anything you can give me."

The arrogance of the young man obviously grated on Princess Merle. "Very well," she snapped, her face reddening. She called to one of the guards. "See that Gaelan here has more work. He apparently has time to gossip with the rest of these men." She set her eyes on Dave then and said, "Do you need more work too?"

"No, I think this is enough for me," Dave said carefully. He had learned that a little humility might go a long way.

After the Princess moved away, Dave and Gaelan

continued talking quietly. He asked Gaelan about the physical possibilities of escape.

Gaelan said finally, "You know, there's another one that I'd like to see come with us."

"Who's that?"

"Rolf, the son of the queen."

"What's he like?"

"Well, believe it or not, he's not a bad fellow. He's been under the thumb of his mother and his sister and these other women for so long that he hardly knows he's a man. But if I could get him away, I could teach him some things." His hazel eyes gleamed with thought. "I don't know if he's got enough nerve to run away, though. They've pretty well drained him of all the manhood he had."

Over the next few days Dave grew very close to Gaelan. He met Rolf also, a wiry and small-boned but tallish young man. He had light blond hair and mild blue eyes.

Carefully Dave tried to suggest that, as the son of the house, he might take more responsibility. But Rolf merely stared at him blankly. "My mother is the queen," he said quietly. "When she dies, my sister, Merle, will be the queen. I help my father with the house."

Well, that takes care of Rolf, unless there's a big change in his life, Dave said to himself.

Later he and Sarah met by accident, both getting water from the stream that flowed through the village.

"How are you doing, Sarah?"

"They're trying to make a warrior maid out of me." She grimaced. "I feel sorry for Josh. Those two women are making life miserable for him."

"I know the feeling."

"I don't think you do. Marden and Ettore, they're a pair of vicious ferrets! They've had Josh whipped twice

87

already, just for minor offenses. When I protested, they said a warrior maid had to be made of tougher stuff." Sarah's eyes glittered. "Ooh, I'd like to get my hands around the necks of those two!"

"Hey, you're beginning to sound pretty blood-thirsty," Dave said with a smile. "I wish we all had some of that toughness. Especially Abbey, but she's just not as strong as you are."

"I know. I've talked to her." Sarah had opportunity to move around more than the guys did, and she gave a report of what she'd learned. "That Tanisha is about to drive Reb crazy. She's already asked him to be her mate."

Dave laughed aloud. "What did Reb do?"

"He turned absolutely pale. You could see his freckles standing out. So far, he's been too shocked to say anything."

"Somehow we've got to get out of this mess. I don't see any way of ever changing these people."

"There's a way. We've just got to find it," Sarah said.

And then the guards moved close and said, "No talking. Get the water and be gone."

"I'll see you later," Dave said. He carried his water pails back to the queen's house, where he found Chava sitting with the queen, reading to her from a book.

After Dave emptied the water, he lingered, listening.

The queen looked at him with her cold eyes. "Are you through there? Then be off."

"Yes, Your Majesty."

"Do you like poetry, boy?" Chava called out.

"I like some of it, although I don't understand it very well."

"Good, you can hear some of mine," Chava said.

When the boy left, Chava said, "He's a fine young man."

Faya had been studying Dave. "He might do as a mate for Merle."

"I don't think she cares for him," Chava offered anxiously. "They don't get along."

"They don't need to get along. She'll be the queen one day. He'll do as she says."

"Yes, Faya."

Queen Faya suddenly looked at her husband, and her eyes softened. "Not every man is like you," she said quietly. She studied the small man sitting beside her, and she said gently, "I could not have held the throne without you, although nobody believes that."

Chava reached over and took her hand. "You are a magnificent leader, Faya. You have held these people together as no one else could."

Queen Faya listened to his words, then closed her eyes and leaned back. With a sigh she said, "I do not know what will become of the throne. Merle must be ready."

"Your reign isn't over for a long time," Chava said. "But," he then added, "if Merle must have a mate, I think that young man would be a good one—if he could learn to accept a few things."

9

Yesterday and Today

One member of the tribe that Dave and Sarah found most interesting was Zuriel, the historian. He was probably between fifty and sixty but seemed older. He had a long gray beard and a bushy head of hair to match. His eyes had wrinkles about them but were bright as a bird's.

Dave and Sarah had found him to be a well of information, and now the two of them had gone to his house and were sitting on the ground in front of him.

Zuriel sat on a low stool, holding a bark tablet. He had put his writing away, however, and for the last hour had been telling them stories of the Kingdom of Fedor.

His knowledge went back past his own days, and he told them, "My father was the historian before me, and his father before him. Some of Fedor's history is written down, but much of it is in songs and in long poems which we've committed to memory."

Sarah listened with such interest that the old man seemed flattered. She said, "Most of the world away from here is not like Fedor."

The man nodded. "All places are different."

"I mean, men and women behave differently there," Sarah said with some hesitation. "Do you know, Zuriel, how *strange* this place is?"

His wise old eyes sharpened, and he looked around as though to see if anyone was near. Children were playing close by, rolling in the dirt, and some guards paced along the walls, but no one could hear his words. Nevertheless, he lowered his voice. "Yes, I know. You speak of how the women are always in charge here and never the men."

Dave leaned forward. "How did that happen? Did it begin in your time?"

"No, it was before the time of my father's father. I heard him tell of it, though. I was a mere child, and he was an old, old man. But like all good storytellers, he told every story exactly the same way every time he told it, and I heard him tell this story more than once. Women think that Fedor has always been like this, but it hasn't."

"How did it change?"

Zuriel bent his head and let old memories pour over him. Then he began to speak in a strange sort of cadence. His young hearers knew he was repeating the story as he had heard it from his grandfather.

"There was a time when the men ruled over the tribe. The women cooked and kept the houses and bore the children. The men went out and hunted game, and they fought when the enemy came to destroy the tribe." He went on, describing normal village life such as Dave and Sarah could imagine.

At last he said, "But then war came, and almost all the men were killed. The women took over. One woman was stronger than the rest. She determined to become queen, and she forced the others to accept her. She formed the strongest women into guards and taught them to fight. The few men that were left were old or very young or wounded. They were practically made servants. This went on all through the queen's life, and she insisted that every time her maidens married, they would rule their households. She taught them the art of war, and they learned well. For generations this went on until today no one can remember when it was different."

When Zuriel finished, Dave said, "Zuriel, we need to turn this village around. It's based on the wrong kind of relationships."

"I do not know about relationships," Zuriel said, shaking his head, "but you would have trouble changing things. Change is always hard."

"Do you think change would be good, Zuriel?" Sarah asked him directly.

"I'm old, and if the queen or her council heard this, they would have me given to the Dark Gods; but yes, I think the custom should be changed. No one should rule to the hurt of someone else."

Zuriel seemed to have shocked even himself, and then his eyes opened wide. "Do not tell me you are thinking of leading a rebellion. We'd all die in the attempt. The women are good warriors; the weaker ones have died. Now only the strong are left."

"All things are possible where Goél is concerned. But tell us about this god you serve. This one you call Maug."

"There is always a Dark God," Zuriel said sadly. "Sometimes his name is something else, but it is always the same dark power. You must have him in your world too."

"Yes, we did." Dave nodded sadly. "But he can be defeated. Goél is stronger."

"That would be a good thing. I would like to see the end of Maug—and to take Mita's beads away from her. She is a mean, vicious woman, responsible for the death of many innocents."

"She'll be the first to go," Sarah said with determination.

They talked for a long time, and Zuriel warned

again, "You cannot take them by force. They're too strong."

"You're right, Zuriel," Sarah said slowly. "We're not strong enough to do that."

"How *can* we do it then?" Dave asked in some bewilderment.

"Remember what Goél said?"

Dave thought for a moment. "You don't mean about love, do you?"

"That's exactly what I mean."

Dave shrugged his shoulders and laughed shortly. "I don't think they'd have much respect for love. All they respect is a sword or an arrow."

"They may be warrior women, but they're women all the same, and though it might be buried very deep, they want love. I'm sure of it."

Dave stared at her with consternation. "Well, Sarah, you're the expert on romance, but how are we going to get them to listen?"

"Somehow we'll find a way." Sarah smiled. She looked up at Zuriel and said, "Now, tell us more. We need to know everything about the nature of these Amazons."

Ettore was watching Josh scrub the floor. A knowing smile touched her lips but not her eyes. She had delighted in tormenting Josh ever since she brought him home, and she now ambled over and leaned against the wall, looking down at him silently.

Josh felt her presence but did not look up. His back still ached from the last beating she had administered with the cane she kept especially for that purpose. He had endured the caning without uttering a sound, but this had seemed to anger Ettore rather than please her, and she had redoubled her efforts. Marden, her mother, finally said, "That's enough. We don't want him scarred up in case we want to sell him."

Now Ettore studied the young man. "Are you afraid to look at me?" she asked.

Josh straightened up. He was kneeling and did not rise to his feet, but his blue eyes met hers without flinching. "No, I'm not afraid to look at you," he said calmly.

"Watch your tone, or you'll get another caning," Ettore warned. "And stand up!" she commanded.

When Josh was standing, she began to prod his arms and chest. Josh's flesh crawled, and he yearned to strike her hands away. He had seen farmers run their hands over cattle they were considering buying. She had to know that he hated to be touched, and she persisted every day in aggravating him in this way. Somehow her touch was degrading to him, but he tried to let none of this show in his face.

Finally Etttore seemed angered that he did not respond. "I've been too easy on you," she said. "You're spoiled."

"If you say so," Josh said, his lips in a straight line, his eyes still locked onto hers.

"Well, aren't you the meek one! I can see what's inside your head, though. You'd like to get at me with a knife, wouldn't you?"

Josh suddenly asked, "Why do you treat me this way? You treat all your servants badly." He knew none of the slaves in the household of Marden and Ettore escaped punishment.

"Quiet!"

But Josh did not obey. "Haven't you looked around?" he asked. "Those people who treat their servants nicely get loyalty out of them. All you get is hatred, because that's all you ever show. It's no way to live."

Ettore cracked him across the cheek with an open hand. The blow made an ugly splat, and her fingers were outlined on his cheek. "I told you to be silent," she said. "You're mine, and I'll do with you as I please. I may even decide to have you as my mate."

"I'd rather have a snake for a mate," Josh said. He knew at once that he had made a mistake.

Rage flickered in Ettore's dark eyes. She whirled and ran through the house yelling, "Where's my cane?"

She found it, came back, and began to beat Josh about the head. Helplessly he stood there, covering his head with his hands. Then the cane burned like fire as it lashed across his back and sides. He was wearing only a thin shirt, and he heard it tear. He tried to ignore the pain, keeping his lips tightly shut and his eyes closed.

"Stop that!"

Josh opened his eyes to see that Sarah had come into the room and had stepped between him and Ettore.

"Get out of my way, Sarah."

"I won't do it. If you have to whip somebody, start in on me."

"I could do that, you know!"

"Why don't you?" Sarah said. "But I warn you, I won't take it like Josh does." She seized a broom and said, "Go ahead. We'll see who gives up first—you with your cane or me with my broom."

Suddenly Ettore laughed. She held the cane in one hand, tapping her other palm with it, and she smiled cruelly. "I like that! You've got fire. You may make a warrior maid after all." She scrutinized the girl and said, "You like him, don't you?"

Sarah flushed. "We've been friends a long time."

"Friends? A woman doesn't need a man for a

friend—just for a mate and then to take care of the house and the children. A woman has more important things to do."

"I don't think so," Sarah said. "I don't think there's anything more important than a husband and children."

Ettore laughed harshly. "You'll change your mind, and don't get your heart set on this one. He's a little skinny right now, but when we fatten him up he may be just what we need." She grabbed Josh by the hair and pulled his head back. "He's not as tough as Dave, but he might do." She gave Josh's hair a cruel twist, laughed at the pain in his eyes, then turned and swaggered out of the room.

Sarah turned to Josh. "I'm sorry. She's an awful person."

"That's putting it mildly." Josh flexed his arm carefully, and a grimace crossed his lips.

"Let me see your back," Sarah said.

"No."

"Don't be foolish, Josh. Let me see. Take off your shirt."

Sarah drew a sharp breath at the welts that crisscrossed his back and sides. "Let me put some ointment on that. It'll take some of the soreness out."

She ran quickly and got her kit. She had some medical supplies—they had allowed her to keep everything except her weapons—and with a hand that trembled slightly she began to anoint the ugly welts.

Josh stood perfectly still. The ointment brought coolness to the burning wounds, and her hands were soft and gentle. When she had finished, he slipped his shirt on, saying with a faint smile, "Thanks, Sarah."

"We've got to do something, Josh," she said almost desperately.

"Do what? We're guarded night and day—even you. They pretend they're going to make a warrior maid out of you, but just try to get away and see what happens."

Sarah bit her lip. "I know. I've been able to talk to Dave. He's talking about escape."

"No, we can't do that! They'd hunt whoever got away like dogs. We don't know our way in this jungle, and they do."

"That's what I told him. Whatever we do, we have to do it together. He did tell me, though, about the queen's son—Rolf. I met him a couple of times. He's a nice boy."

"Boy? He's nearly twenty, isn't he?"

"I know, but he seems so . . . well . . . vulnerable. Dave's been working on him some. And then there's a young man called Gaelan. There are others, I am sure. If we could get enough men together—"

Josh stared at her. "You mean to take over from these Amazons? *That* would take some doing."

"I know. It's just that we need to be doing *something*. I'm going to talk to Rolf now. At least he has the queen's ear."

"From what I hear, Queen Faya doesn't listen to anybody."

"I don't think that's true," Sarah said slowly. "I've watched them quite a bit, and I've talked to Abbey about it. She listens to her husband. I think she trusts him more than anybody."

"He's still just a husband—she's the queen."

"That's true. Well, that's the culture here, and that's what's got to be broken before they can understand anything about love."

Sarah found Rolf working in the garden in the sun-

98

light. He had removed his shirt, and she was surprised to see that he was not feeble looking but wiry. And as he dug with the hoe, the muscles of his sides and shoulders sprang into instant relief.

"Hello, Rolf," she said.

"Oh, hello, Sarah." Rolf smiled at her. He had a pleasant smile. "How are things going over at Marden's?"

"Well, they're pretty strict, especially with Josh."

"Yes, everybody knows that. They beat their servants all the time." He shook his head. "That's a bad idea. Why make life hard for people?"

There was a gentle streak in this young man that Sarah warmed to. She watched as he hoed, noting that he did it effortlessly and quickly. "You do that so well," she said.

"I ought to. I've been doing it all my life."

"Do you ever wish, Rolf, that you could do something else?"

"Something else?" He raised one eyebrow. "What else would I do?"

"Well, I mean, have you ever wanted to go hunting?"

"I suppose I did when I was younger." A memory seemed to come to him, and his eyes grew dreamy. "When I was a boy, I used to pretend I was hunting. The women would go out and bring the game back, and I thought, *I'd like to do that.* But, of course, I never did. Merle, she's a good hunter."

"I think you'd be a good hunter yourself. You're strong and quick, and you probably have good eyes."

"Oh, I don't know about that—"

Sarah had recognized earlier that Rolf had a very low self-image. It had been ground into him since he was born that he was inferior, and Sarah knew that was hard to work against. She had had a poor view of herself when she was a child. She had felt herself to be homely and thought no one would ever like her.

Childhood had been a hard time for her, and now, looking at the sinewy young man working in the garden, she thought, *He could be a strong man if he just had some encouragement. I've got to be careful though —he'd be easy to shock. If I told him I would like to see the men take over from the women warriors, he'd probably run like a rabbit.*

She spent a pleasant half hour with Rolf, then made her way over to the house where Reb and Wash stayed with Tanisha and her parents.

She saw Wash almost at once and asked, "Where's Reb?"

"He's hiding," Wash said, rolling his eyes upward.

"Hiding? Hiding from whom?"

"From that girl who chases him everywhere. That Tanisha."

Sarah could not help smiling. "Well, I guess he's flattered that she likes him."

"No, he isn't." Wash shook his head definitively. "She's about to drive him crazy. Every time he turns around, she's right there picking at him. I think she's already proposed to him."

"You mean she wants to *marry* him?"

"She don't talk about marrying. She just wants him to be her 'mate.' That's the way she put it." Wash shook his head grimly. "That ain't no way for folks to behave. I'm plumb worried about Reb."

"Have you seen Jake?"

"Yeah, he's right next door over there. I guess he's no worse off than the rest of us. The folks that took him in are pretty easygoing. They're a little bit older than most. I expect we'll get to talk to him a lot. All he talks about is getting some gunpowder and blowing up this whole village!"

"I don't guess that'll do. I need to talk to Reb."

Wash leaned closer, "Well, you have to find him. He's over there behind them buildings. That's where they do the tanning. Don't tell Tanisha, though. I think Reb's about ready to jump the wall if she don't leave him alone."

"I won't tell her." Sarah made her way to the tanning sheds, where she found Reb sitting behind them, looking miserable.

"Reb," she said. Then, when he jumped up, she said quickly, "No, I didn't bring Tanisha."

"Good! That female is going to drive me crazy. You know what she wants to do?"

"I heard."

"Ain't that an awful thing to think about?" Reb groaned. "What am I going to do, Sarah?"

"I take it you're not contemplating marriage?"

"Are you crazy? That female would drive me absolutely up a tree! I got to get out of here, that's all there is to it."

"I know—it's bad over where we are too. Something's got to happen and happen quick."

Reb looked at her hopefully. "Why don't we try to bust out of here? I talked to Dave, and he's about ready to make a break."

"We can't do that," Sarah said. "They'd run us down in no time in the jungle. You know that. We'll just have to wait."

"I reckon that's right, but something better happen quick."

10
The Game

As the days stretched on, life became more and more miserable for the Sleepers. The girls had it better in many respects, for they were treated with some consideration. None of the young men, though, had anything good happen to them.

In desperation, and to break the monotony, it was Dave who suggested on one of their afternoons off, "Why don't we play a little touch football?"

His suggestion caught on, and Jake fashioned a sort of football out of leather and stuffed it with moss. It did not look a great deal like a football, but when he tossed it to Dave, Dave put his fingers on the seam and threw a long, spiraling pass to Reb, who caught it easily.

"Too bad we don't have enough people for a real game," Dave said.

But soon they were lined up, playing and forgetting their troubles. It was a fairly even match, for Dave could throw a pass better than anyone else, and Reb could catch anything that came into his area.

There was a lot of laughter, and since there was little to do at that time of the afternoon, quite a few village men gathered around to watch. The game intrigued them.

"Some of you guys want to play?"

"Yes." Gaelan stepped up, and Rolf was right behind him. Soon they gathered enough players for two teams.

It became obvious that Rolf was a natural-born

athlete. He had quicker reflexes than anyone the Sleepers had ever seen.

"Boy, you'd be great at any sport," Josh said with admiration after Rolf caught a pass and, dodging and weaving, outran everybody to score.

"Sport? What is that?"

"This is sport. Playing games."

"It is fun," Rolf said. "Let's play some more."

The games went on at free time for a couple of days, and even the women gathered to watch. Ettore made rude remarks concerning the abilities of the men, and on the third day, Josh said, "Why don't you ladies get a team together, and we'll show you how good we are."

"It would be no contest," Ettore sniffed. "You could not beat the women."

"Why don't you try, Ettore?" Rolf asked. "It would be fun."

Ettore glared at him, then she laughed. "All right, we will show you a thing or two." She saw Princess Merle and said, "Come, Princess. You and I, we will lead."

Merle laughed. She loved games of every sort and quickly chose the fastest and the most agile of the maids for their team. "Now, how do you play this stupid game?" she asked.

"It's real simple," Dave said. He explained the rules, then said, "We'll just try a few plays to show you how it goes."

The warrior maids were all excellent athletes. They were fast and learned rapidly.

Finally Dave said innocently, "All right, you take the ball, and we'll let you have the first chance to score."

The women had already found out that Ettore had

the strongest arm and that she could throw fairly accurately. She had practiced for some time on the sidelines. Now she laughed and said, "Let's show these weakling men what it is to play against warrior maids."

She called a huddle as she had seen the men do. "Princess, you run over to the right. I will throw you the ball. The rest of you go before her. If anyone gets in your way, smash them down." A happy laugh went up, and the maidens ran back.

"This is called the line of scrimmage," Dave said. "Remember, no tackling—this is touch. You just touch the one with the ball, and that's where the ball is dead."

Ettore paid him no attention. She called for the ball, and it came back to her from the center.

Only Dave and Reb stayed back to guard against the pass. The rest of the boys rushed forward. Jake was knocked instantly on his back after taking an elbow in the throat. Wash had his feet kicked out from under him and fell to the ground with a shrill cry. All down the line, the warrior maids used every tactic they could to slow down the men. Only Rolf got through the line by slipping quickly past the maid who tried to stop him. He was almost to Ettore when she let the ball go. Then she turned and slashed him across the forehead with an arm.

"That's wasn't necessary," Rolf explained. "When you throw the ball, there's no danger."

"Go on, Rolf. Get back with the weaklings."

Ettore was watching the ball. She had thrown a fine pass to Merle, and two of the maids were out in front of the princess. They saw Dave and Reb rushing to touch her, and they screamed, "Kill them!" Instantly the two of them took Reb down, one high and one low. He rolled in the dust but yelled, "You got her, Dave!"

Dave rushed forward, and, since there was no one

in front of him, he simply tagged Merle. She ignored this, struck him in the stomach, and kicked his feet out from under him. Then she ran on and triumphantly hollered, "We win!"

The women were all laughing, for the men were lying in various stages of injury.

"Now it's your turn. See what you can do," Princess Merle said mockingly, tossing the ball to Dave, who had gotten slowly to his feet.

"I take it you don't want to play *touch* football," he said.

"We warrior maids take any advantage we can."

"Fine," Dave said. "Just wanted to be sure about the rules."

He called his team back into a huddle and said, "Those are pretty rough ladies, and they want to call off the easy stuff."

"What does that mean?" Rolf said, a puzzled light in his eyes.

"It means we hit them hard. Go right over them if you can."

This troubled Rolf, but Gaelan laughed aloud. "Let me do a little of that."

Dave grinned at him. "Fine, Gaelan. When I get the ball, I'm going to run with it. You and Reb stay right in front of me. Anybody that gets in my way, knock them down."

"Even if it's the Princess?" Rolf said, shocked.

"She made up the rules." Dave grinned and winked at Reb. "You got it?"

"I reckon so. We'll take 'em like Stonewall Jackson took Grant."

"I don't remember that bit of history—" Dave smiled "—but let's show these gals what it's like."

The young women were waiting, laughing and

talking and jeering as though they had been planning their own strategy. As soon as the ball was snapped, several of them picked up dirt and threw it into their opponents' faces.

Once again, Wash and Jake went to the ground. Josh had centered the ball but dodged the dirt that came at him. A large maiden started for him, but Josh ducked under her arms, striking her in the stomach with his shoulder. He heard, with satisfaction, the *whoosh* as she fell to the ground.

As soon as he got the ball, Dave started to his right. Several warriors were running to cut him off, but he got behind Reb and Gaelan, who ran with determination in front of him. "Cut 'em down, guys," he yelled.

The first tackler was Ettore. She attempted to strike Reb across the eye. He simply launched himself in the air and caught her across the knees. She fell to the ground with a thump, as if she had been cut down with a scythe. She did not get up at once.

Another tackler came toward Gaelan. He yelled loudly and struck her right in the middle, propelling her backward.

Dave saw at a glance that only Princess Merle stood in his way. The light of battle was in her eyes. She ran straight at him, her hands outstretched—to catch him by the head, it seemed. Dave did not hesitate a moment. He was strongly built and outweighed her by at least thirty pounds. She tried gamely, but she might as well have been trying to stop a rampaging buffalo. He charged, she flew backward, and he leaped over her.

When he reached the goal line, he turned back and watched as she rolled over. Her face was covered with dirt, and some of it had gotten into her mouth. She spit it out and got to her feet unsteadily.

"That was pretty good for a girl," Dave said casually.

Fury came over Princess Merle, and she glanced around to see that some in the crowd were hiding smiles. "We'll try that again," she said angrily.

"Sure, it's your turn. Here's the ball."

Dave walked back to where the men were rejoicing. The light of battle was in Gaelan's eyes now, and he said, "That did me more good than anything I've ever done. Let me take a crack at 'em this time."

Rolf said, "I'm not sure about this. It doesn't seem right, playing this way. I thought this was supposed to be a fun game."

"It is," Dave said. "It's the warrior maids who want to play rough, but I don't think they'll last long at it."

The maids tried hard, but they were not practiced and knew no techniques. At least three of the men—Josh, Reb, and Dave—had played varsity football. They ran roughshod over their opponents, and soon the game became a runaway.

On the other hand, the whole thing was a mistake, which Jake saw more quickly than anyone else. "Hey," he said in one of their huddles, "I like to see those babes get it, but it's not going to be any fun when they get their licks back on us—and they will, you know."

He was right about that. After the game was over, the sullen women retreated to their houses, but from that day forth they made life totally miserable for the young men.

A quarrel broke out between Princess Merle and Rolf. She was so angry at everything male that she shoved him out of her way, and Chava said, "What's the matter with you, Merle? That's no way to treat your brother."

Merle turned and without thinking cried, "Oh, be still!" And then her eyes flew wide, for she had always spoken respectfully to her father. She remembered that he had always been good to her, and now she recognized the hurt in his eyes.

Quickly she looked to her mother, Queen Faya, who was staring at her with a strange expression. "Why do you treat your brother and your father like this? Is it because you were beaten in that silly game?"

"No, that has nothing to do with it!" Merle said, but she made no one believe it. She whirled and walked out of the house. If ever Princess Merle was close to tears, this was the time. She was angry with herself and angry with everyone else.

Things went badly for Josh too. He was beaten twice in the next three days by Ettore, and there was nothing Sarah could do to stop it. She wanted to tell him that it had been foolish to humiliate the women, but it was too late to say anything about that now.

"We'll just have to wait until they get over it," she whispered to him after his second beating.

"They'll never get over it," he said bitterly.

Secretly Sarah thought he might be right, but there was nothing more to say.

Later that evening there was a small meeting of the women, including Marden and four others, who served as the queen's council. They stood before Faya, who listened as they brought their reports.

It was an open meeting, and everyone in the village was welcome to come. The men, of course, had to keep in the background. The Sleepers, by common consent, came together. Josh, Reb, Dave, Jake, and Wash felt secure being there, and right across from them Sarah and Abbey stood listening to what went on.

Most of the business was run-of-the-mill, but then a shrill voice arose. The Sleepers turned to see Mita, the medicine woman, come out of the crowd of listeners, shaking her charms. She spoke for a long time, and Reb said, "I reckon she's about ready to turn her wolf loose."

"Yeah," Jake said, "and I think I know who she's aiming that wolf at. The old woman's been lookin' at us, and if I ever saw an evil eye, she's got it."

Jake was not mistaken, for now the discussion turned on Mita's prophecy.

She moved in front of the Seven Sleepers, lifting her arms and her clawlike hands. "These are bad people. Maug does not like them. They will bring bad luck on the village." She continued her tirade for some time, then went back to stand before the queen. "Maug demands a sacrifice. Kill them and get rid of the danger. You know Maug is strong."

"We have kept captives before," Queen Faya said slowly. Her eyes went over to study the Seven Sleepers, and she shook her head. "They are valuable property."

Mita's voice rose into a scream of rage. "Kill them!" she said. "Some of our people will die if we do not offer a sacrifice to Maug. You will see! You will see!"

Apparently her screams almost convinced Queen Faya. She glanced at her husband, who shook his head slightly.

Nobody seemed to see that except Sarah and Dave. Their eyes met, and they nodded.

After the meeting was over, Faya was helped back to her house by some of her attendants. When she was inside and on her couch, she motioned for Dave and the other servants to leave.

Then she turned to Chava. "You heard what Mita said?"

"Yes, I heard."

"It could be true. Perhaps Maug *is* angry."

"Mita is always saying that Maug is angry. If we killed somebody as a sacrifice every time she opened her mouth, we'd have nobody left in the village."

Doubt crossed Queen Faya's features. She was in severe pain with her leg tonight, and quickly Chava prepared a potion that would give her some ease. She drank it quickly and lay back. "Read to me some of your poems," she said quietly.

Chava picked up the awkward-looking book that he had made out of thin bark and written on with homemade ink. He began to read, and he saw his wife's eyes slowly closing. When she was almost asleep, he said, "Do not let Mita and the others cause you to be unjust."

"No, Chava," she said. She opened her eyes with an effort, smiled at him, and then dropped off.

Chava took the book and went outside, where he found Dave and Abbey speaking quietly together. They looked up as he approached, and he said with a worried air, "I'm afraid Mita's up to mischief."

"Isn't she always?" Dave asked bitterly. "The old witch!"

"You speak more truly than you know," Chava said. "She is, indeed, in the power of darkness. Can't you feel the evil? It seeps out of her and infects everyone she touches." He looked at the pair. "She has a special hatred for you. I think it is your master, Goél, that she hates."

"We find the Dark Lord has agents everywhere we go," Abbey said quietly. "Do you think the queen will listen to her?"

"Not unless something terrible happens."

"Well, let's hope it doesn't," Dave said fervently. "I didn't like the look in that old witch's eyes!"

11
Tigers

Gaelan went about his work after the football game, but there was hope in him that had not been there before. The fame of the warrior maids had spread throughout his world, so that they had seemed invincible. Many of his people had been kidnapped into slavery by the women of Fedor. However, since he had seen their finest warriors tumbled in the dust, his heart sang within him. And now as he moved along the row he was hoeing, he said to himself, *They* aren't *invincible. This won't last forever. Sooner or later I'll be free!*

After he had finished hoeing the beans, he shouldered his hoe and ambled down to the laundry area where some men had gathered to wash clothes again. He saw Rolf and joined him. "How about another football game, Rolf?" he whispered, nudging him in the ribs.

Rolf grinned at him unexpectedly.

Gaelan knew Rolf had been troubled by the violence of the game. He was the mildest of young men. But seemingly, in the rough and tumble, Rolf had found a fiery spirit of competition within himself that shocked him.

"Well, I expect we could play among ourselves, but you took plenty of punishment from my sister over the last game, didn't you?"

"It was worth it." Gaelan grinned back. "But maybe you're right," he added quietly. "Someday we may be able to do things a little better."

"A little better?" Rolf said, a puzzled light in his eyes. "What do you mean by that?"

"Haven't you noticed, Rolf, that everything is all wrong here? I mean, women aren't really more able than men."

"Why, of course they are! The maidens are the warriors."

"Only because that's the custom. Did you see how easily you put some of them on their backs? They didn't look like warrior maids then, did they?"

"Well, maybe not, but hunting is different from playing a game."

"Not really," Gaelan said easily.

Gaelan had been talking with Dave and Sarah, and the three of them agreed that Rolf could, perhaps, be the key to their freedom. If they proved to him that men were qualified to soldier and rule, the battle would be half won.

Rolf said slowly, "It's always been like this. I don't think it can be any different. Look at my father—he couldn't rule the way that my mother has. He's just not the right type."

"Maybe not. Some men aren't. But you are."

"Me?" Rolf stared at him, genuinely shocked. "Why, I couldn't rule the country!"

"Only because you don't *think* you can. Look, Rolf, you can run faster, lift more weight, and with a little training, with your coordination, you could shoot straighter than anyone. Have you ever done any sword fighting?"

"Well, as a matter of fact, I have fenced with Merle a little bit."

"I bet you could've beaten her too." At the look that crossed Rolf's face, Gaelan grinned. "I thought so. You didn't do it because she was your sister and she was a woman, but if you'd gone all out you could've bested her, couldn't you?"

The idea seemed to be novel. He let Rolf think about it awhile.

"Perhaps I could," he said slowly, "but I wouldn't do that to my sister."

"You might be doing her a favor. From what I hear, anytime the Londo tribe attacks, you're liable to get wiped out. Isn't that true?"

Gaelan had hit upon a touchy subject, for Ulla, chief of the Londos, had sworn to obliterate the women of Fedor. He had fierce warriors, and in several pitched battles the warrior maids had barely managed to stave off defeat. They had lost large numbers of their best warriors, and now the threat of an attack from the Londos hung over the entire village, although it was not publicly spoken of.

Rolf said nothing, but Gaelan saw that his mind was working rapidly. He was, Gaelan knew, a quick-thinking young man, with a razor-sharp mind, although he had never fully used it.

Gaelan stood there with him on the riverbank as he stirred clothes, idly talking about nothing but dropping ideas into Rolf's mind. Finally, when he thought it was wise, he said, "We'll talk about this later."

"All right, Gaelan."

Gaelan made his way back to the queen's home, where he put his hoe into the shed, then walked toward the house.

When he entered, he was met by Princess Merle. He had knocked her flat on her back once during the football game, and he knew she had never forgiven him for it.

Her eyes flashed now as she said, "Where have

you been? You were supposed to be here to help Father."

"I was hoeing beans, and then I went down to the river and talked with your brother."

"You've got more to do than trade useless stories with Rolf."

"I don't know that they were useless. Your brother is a pretty sharp young fellow." He grinned widely. "And a pretty good ball player too."

Princess Merle's face flushed at the mention of the game. She flared up. "Don't you stand there laughing at me!"

"I wasn't laughing," Gaelan protested, drawing his face into a frown. He suspected this made him look ridiculous, and he realized he couldn't hold it. He laughed suddenly, saying, "Well, I couldn't help it. You *were* funny rolling around in the dirt. But then, I rolled some myself."

At the reference to being flattened, Merle's temper erupted. Her hand flashed out.

She did not strike Gaelan's face, however, for he had reflexes faster than hers. He grabbed her wrist. She struggled to free herself, but he held her effortlessly. She slapped at him with her other hand, but then this was pinioned too. She stood there struggling, her face growing redder, and he smiled across at her, holding her easily as he would a child.

"Let me go! I'll kill you!" she said.

"I don't doubt that."

"What's this?" Queen Faya stumped in through the door, holding onto her crutch. She took in the scene and said, "What's this man doing?"

"He insulted me, Queen Mother."

Gaelan released the princess's wrist. "I merely kept her from striking me, Your Majesty."

"Why would she want to strike you?"

"That I can't say."

"He's impudent, that's why. He needs a thrashing, and I'm going to give it to him."

"Are you?" Queen Faya asked, raising her eyebrows. She herself did not believe that beating servants and slaves accomplished a great deal. "I don't think you'll find that satisfactory."

But Merle's blood was up. "Come along," she said. "You're going to get a caning."

Gaelan exchanged a steady glance with the queen and for some reason smiled. "Excuse me, Your Majesty, your daughter has . . . business with me."

Gaelan's manner had amused Queen Faya, but she said no more. She hobbled to a chair and sat down, staring out a window. Soon she heard the sound of blows being administered in another room.

When Merle returned, she was flushed and unhappy-looking.

"Well, did that make you feel better, Daughter?"

"Yes!"

"I doubt that. Come and sit down by me. We need to talk."

Reluctantly Princess Merle sat down by her mother. Actually she had a great affection for both her parents; but she was about to receive a lecture, and she pulled her lips together in a thin line, determined not to hear anything.

"You are a very strong-willed young woman, which is as it should be," Queen Faya said gently. There was a faraway look in her eye, and she smiled. "I was exactly like you when I was seventeen years old. Not as pretty as you, though."

"Yes, you were," Merle insisted loyally.

"No, I was not. Many men wanted me for their mate, but it was only because I was the queen. Only your father loved me for what I was besides being queen."

"How did you know that? You never told me how you and he met."

"He was just a commoner, and at the time I was a princess as you are now. He was the smartest of all the young men, though not the best-looking. He never spoke to me, but I felt his eyes on me," Faya said quietly, remembering old days. "There were others who were larger and stronger, but none had the look in their eyes that your father had."

"So how did you come to choose him?"

"I found a poem that he had written. He didn't know that I'd found it. It was a wonderful poem. I still have it."

"Could I see it?"

"No, it was a very private love poem that he wrote for me—the only one I ever got," Faya said. She looked at her daughter. "I don't suppose you've gotten any love poems?"

"No, I—I think they're silly."

"Then you've missed an education." The queen looked sad and for a time remained silent. "I think most of our young warrior maids miss something fine and wonderful. Your father is a quiet man, and he doesn't say much, but for years I have not made a decision without his counsel. Does that surprise you?"

"N-no," Merle said slowly. "I've always known you two were closer than any couple in the tribe, but I didn't know why."

Queen Faya took her daughter's hand and held it. "It's because he has love and gentleness. Our women have little of that. They are trained to be fierce warriors; and I think when a woman becomes a warrior, she loses something."

"But it's what I've always wanted to be."

"It's what I've taught you to want—what the others have urged upon you. But inside there is a beautiful woman who wants to be loved and to be told that she's pretty and to be admired."

Amazed, Merle could not speak. As her mother went on, suddenly, to her surprise and shock and horror, she felt tears rising to her eyes. Her mother was saying the things that had lain deep in Merle's own heart for years, thoughts she'd felt disloyal to speak. She turned her head away, but her mother saw that she was weeping.

"Never be ashamed of your tears, my dear," she said quietly. "If our women could learn to cry, they would be more complete. It's all right to weep. I do it myself sometimes."

"Mother, why have you never talked to me like this before?"

"Because I'm weak," Queen Faya said, shaking her head. "I've known the truth—that our women are not gentle and therefore are not fully women. Women *should* be strong, and they *should* stand with courage, but we've bred ourselves to be nothing but fierce animals, knowing nothing but fighting and killing. It's the men who have the gentleness—men like your brother, Rolf, who's like your father. And that young man that you just beat, he has courage like a steel bar—I see it in him—but there's a gentleness and a goodness in him too."

"No, I don't believe that!"

"Don't you? Then you're not a woman yet, or else we've bred all that out of you."

119

"Mother, I don't want to hear any more of this."

"No, people don't want to hear the truth, but you know in your heart that what I am saying is so."

Princess Merle jumped up and left the room. She passed Gaelan, who was sitting outside on a bench. He looked up at her, and their eyes met. He said nothing, but there was no anger in his eyes, as she had expected. It would have been better if he were angry, she thought. His very silence and refusal to rebuke her hurt worse than if he had struck her. She walked blindly away.

Within a week after the football game, the young men had suffered almost all they thought possible.

Josh, Reb, Wash, and Jake were working out in the common fields under the hot sun when suddenly screams came from outside the stockade. They watched the guards run to the small portholes, trying to see what was going on. Then the screams faded away.

"What was *that?* It sounded like a child," Josh said.

"It was a child," Gaelan said, his face grim.

"What was the matter with him?"

"Probably a wild beast."

Gaelan was right, for word soon spread inside the compound that a small girl, eight years old, had been seized by a huge tiger, who had simply snatched her up and dragged her away into the depths of the jungle.

Instantly the village was alerted. The tiger could not get inside, but they well knew what their future held.

"When a beast like that finds the compound," Rolf explained, "and once he's tasted human flesh, he's there forever. That's how the queen got mauled. She led a charge against the biggest tiger anybody had ever seen. She killed him too, but not before he ruined her leg." His face clouded. "No one person ever stood up to a tiger. The whole tribe goes together to run them out. Even the men go as beaters to drive the tiger into the warriors' spears."

"Why don't you trap him!" Jake demanded.

"How do you do that?"

"Well, lots of ways," Jake said. "Dig a hole, let him fall into it. Rig a snare, so that he strangles. Lots of way to kill tigers."

"We know none of those ways," Rolf said. "Besides, the women would think that was cowardly."

The immediate result of the child's death reflected directly on the Sleepers. It was Mita, of course, who went through the village screaming that her prophecy had been fulfilled.

"Kill the Sleepers," she said. "Kill these strangers in our midst. They bring the wrath of Maug down upon us!" Her cry went on until the villagers were upset.

The queen finally came and took her throne, and everyone in the village gathered before her.

Mita was in her element. She spun around, pointing a bony finger at the Sleepers, repeating her prophecy that they must die before Maug would be appeased.

A long debate developed, with Faya reluctant to condemn any of the young people. However, she had been queen a long time, and she read her people well. She caught her husband's eye, and Chava shook his head, but this time she could not refuse. The pressure was too strong.

"You cannot have them all for Maug, Mita. But you can have that one." She pointed at Wash.

At once a cry went up from Sarah. "No, Queen Faya, you can't do it! He hasn't done anything."

"One must die to save the village. That is the way it is," Queen Faya said heavily. She got to her feet and hobbled off with her crutch. Her husband followed, trying to reason with her. But the queen was stubbornly set on this thing. "We must let her have her way with one, or she will have them all," she said.

The other Sleepers watched as Wash was taken away to be imprisoned.

"We can't let them do it, Josh," Dave said.

"I know, but what can we do?"

A silence went over the group until, strangely enough, Jake, the least combative of all—except perhaps for Wash himself—said, "We can kill that tiger."

"We don't know anything about hunting tigers," Josh said. Then he nodded. "But I guess we can learn. Come on, let's go tell the queen."

They could not get in to see the queen immediately. When they finally were admitted, she was resting on her bed, and obviously her leg was paining her. Chava and Merle were at her bedside.

"What do you want?" she asked. "I cannot spare the life of your companion."

"We do not know your ways well, Your Majesty," Josh said, "but we have come to offer you our help."

"Your help? What can you do?"

"We can kill the tiger."

Faya stared at them, then laughed harshly. "You do not know these tigers."

"We had tigers in our own world."

"The tigers of Fedor are not like other animals." She reached back over her shoulder and pointed to the robe that she wore at ceremonial functions. "Have you ever seen claws like those?"

The Sleepers leaned forward to see, and Reb said with a choked voice, "*I* never saw claws like that!"

They were enormous claws, at least four inches long. Such a beast would weigh seven or eight hundred pounds and be almost impossible to stop.

Then Josh thought of the many times that Goél had spoken of courage and of love for one another. He said slowly, "If we all die saving our friend, so be it, but we claim the right, Your Majesty."

Princess Merle's eyes grew wide as she heard what Josh had to say, but she said nothing. She turned to her mother to see what the answer would be.

The room was silent, and Queen Faya was silent for so long that everyone grew nervous. She looked at her husband, who nodded slightly, then she turned to the Sleepers. "Courage is what we value most. But you cannot kill the tiger. Our whole village has gone against these beasts before. You see this leg? It was well and strong as the other, but that day the tiger killed seven of our people and ruined my life forever. I can no longer lead my people in battle," she said. "You are young and inexperienced. It's certain death for you."

"Nevertheless, we will go." Dave's eyes locked with Princess Merle's, and he smiled coldly. "We will see what we can do. We owe Goél our lives, and if death comes, why, so it comes."

"I like that very much," Faya said surprisingly and smiled at the tall young man. "It might well be said by a warrior queen. You shall go against the tiger. Lay your plans well. You may choose any weapons. For the time being, your friend will be free." She fell back then and closed her eyes.

The Sleepers bowed, turned, and left. As soon as they were outside, Josh said, "Well, we got permission. Now all we have to do is get that tiger!"

12

The Plot Thickens

Josh managed to endure the hardship at the house of Marden and her daughter, Ettore—but only barely. He was usually sore from a caning, and he worked long hours. After the football game, Ettore had turned more vicious than usual, and nothing he could do would stop the torment. Sarah did the best she could to stand between the two, but she had little power.

Once Marden herself expressed surprise at the hardness in her daughter. "If you don't like this Josh, why don't we sell him? You can keep the girl for a handmaid if you like."

"No, I'm going to break his will. He's going to do what I want him to do sooner or later."

Marden narrowed her eyes. "I don't think so. I've seen a few like him in my time. This one—even though he's lean and young—has a hard core of determination in him. You may kill him, but I don't think you'll break him."

The two were alone, and it was late. The slaves and servants were all in bed. Ettore seemed nervous. Finally she said, "Mother, the queen is growing weaker all the time, and everyone knows it."

"So what of that?" Marden said carefully. "My sister is older than I, and naturally she is weak. It's a wonder she's alive, after being mauled by that tiger."

"Sooner or later she will die, then *you* will be queen," Ettore said with a crafty smile. "When you're the queen, I will be the princess."

"No, if the queen, my sister, died, Merle would be Queen Mother of Fedor. You know that."

Something crossed Ettore's face, and she remained silent for a while. "But if something happened to Merle also?"

"Then I would be queen. But what could happen?"

"Many things. Warrior maids die all the time. A tiger could take her, or a bear, or a snake. She might be killed or captured in battle. Oh, I wish she—" She broke off suddenly, but her mother read her thought.

"You wish she hadn't escaped the clutches of Ulla and the Londos. I've thought of that myself. But she did."

"But there'll be other battles. You're not satisfied with the way your sister rules, are you, Mother?"

"She's too soft and weak. She listens to that husband of hers too much. When your father was alive, he knew his place. You didn't catch me asking *his* opinion on anything," she snorted.

"You'd make a wonderful queen," Ettore said. "So firm and strong."

"I've always felt I could rule Fedor better than Faya, but I've never had the chance."

The two talked long into the night.

For several days after the discussion with her mother, Ettore thought of little else but the possibility of becoming a part of the ruling family of Fedor. She was a quick-witted young woman with a streak of cruelty in her. She waited until late one night and spoke again to Marden. "I have a plan, Mother."

"A plan for what?"

"If we're going to rule this country, we can't just wait for it to happen. Merle is young. She'll last a long time after her mother dies. We have to—take steps."

Marden's eyes clouded. "What do you mean, 'take steps'?"

Ettore leaned forward. "I know the queen, and you know her even better. What would happen if Ulla and the Londos attack the tribe?"

For a long moment the older woman thought. Her eyes narrowed, and she said, "I see what you mean. Faya is crippled, but she would not be left behind. She would have herself carried into battle."

"And she would not last long, would she? She would be unable to fight. An arrow or a sword would take her."

"Of course, that's right, and that daughter of hers would die rather than leave her."

"Exactly. You see what I'm getting at. Ulla took many losses during the last war, but he would come again if he thought he had a chance. What we have to do," Ettore whispered, "is to make him come."

"What would make him do that?"

"We could get word to him that the tribe is weak—that many of the warrior maids are sick."

"That could bring him all right—" Marden nodded slowly "—but could we win?"

"We are stronger than Ulla thinks. We would be waiting for him. We could have him come into the valley, and we'd put the queen in the forefront, where she will surely want to be. She would be surrounded by Princess Merle and some of her most valiant warrior maids. But we could arrange things so that Ulla knew this. He would throw his full strength against that point. Then—" her eyes glittered in the semidarkness "—after Ulla kills the queen and her daughter, we'll come against him with our full strength and defeat him. Then we can take over all of Ulla's land. You would rule over two kingdoms, but you would appoint me queen of one. We could rule together as queens."

Ettore knew that, underneath, her mother was a greedy woman. Marden had resented her sister's pre-eminence for years. Now Ettore was offering a way to turn things around.

"It would be wicked to do this thing," her mother said slowly.

"But Queen Faya is an old woman. She must die soon in any case. All we are doing is seeing that Fedor has proper leadership. That brat of a daughter of hers could never lead anything! Underneath all her bluster she's a weak woman. She's romantic—I've seen it. Why, she's half in love with that slave! What's his name? Gaelan! Everybody knows it, though she tries to keep it covered up."

For a long time Ettore talked earnestly, and finally she felt a surge of triumph as her mother came slowly to her side.

"Very well," Marden whispered. "I will see that Ulla gets word of our so-called weakness. We will have one of our number pretend to be a betrayer. Lika would be a good one. She's shifty enough to pull it off and is a good actress."

"Make sure she understands and that we know when Ulla is coming. And make sure she leads them to come through the valley by the river. That way, when Ulla has killed the queen and the princess, we can over-whelm him." She leaned back and laughed softly. "I'm going to enjoy being queen," she said. "I think I was born for it!"

Reb and Wash did their best to stay out of Tanisha's way. Wash found that fairly easy, but the chubby young woman seemed to have an unerring ability to dig out Reb, no matter how well he hid himself.

In desperation the two went on a wood-chopping detail. They volunteered mostly to get away from Tanisha. They were accompanied by a guard, an older woman with a stern face. She carried a bow and said, "If you try to run, you won't get far."

Reb looked out at the trackless jungle. "Run where?" he asked. "Come on, Wash, let's start cutting wood."

When it started to grow dark, they loaded their short lengths of wood onto the cart and started back the half mile to the village. The cart trundled along, creaking. Pulling it along, the two young men spoke seldom, for they were tired.

Reb was thinking, with disgust, how Tanisha would greet him. "She doesn't want to be a warrior," he muttered. "She wants to be cuddled, and that's something I can't set out to do."

Wash grinned. "She's a pretty big gal to be cuddled."

"She's all right—not mean like Ettore or some of these other women—but it's just not for me. What do you think—"

Suddenly their guard let out a sharp cry.

Reb had time only to turn. He saw a huge animal covering the ground in what seemed to be impossible leaps.

"It's a tiger!" Reb yelled. "Run, Wash!" He broke into a sprint, and the small black boy was right beside him.

"We can't outrun that thing. I never saw such a tiger—did you see the teeth on him!" Wash gasped.

Reb risked a glance backward. The tiger was at least twice as large as any tiger he had ever seen in a zoo. Beside that, he had two enormous tusks in his

129

upper jaw. "A saber-toothed tiger, that's what he is! I didn't think there was any of them left!"

Then he had no time to talk. The two of them ran with all their strength.

Reb was sure the tiger would get them. He risked one more look.

He saw that the warrior maid had stood her ground. She had notched an arrow to her bow and got off one shot. It struck the tiger in the haunch but did not seriously hurt him. He uttered a mighty roar, and then while the poor warrior maid was trying to notch another arrow, he was upon her.

She uttered a shrill scream that stopped abruptly, and Reb saw with horror that the tiger had probably killed her instantly. He picked her up in his powerful jaws and dragged her off into the trees.

They raced back to the village gate and yelled. It opened immediately. When the gatekeeper demanded to know where their guard was, Reb gasped, "The tiger, he got her! He's out there!"

"I know what this means," Wash said. "That old witch is gonna want to kill somebody."

"I reckon that's right," Reb said. "And that means tomorrow we go huntin' tigers!"

13

The Lady or the Tiger

The death of the warrior maid brought the matter of a sacrifice into fine focus. Naturally, Mita and several of her close companions petitioned the queen.

"You promised we would have the sacrifice. And now we have lost one of our own. It's time to give Maug a sacrifice."

Sadness was on Faya's face. She looked over to the Sleepers and said, "You must now fulfill your word. Either you kill the tiger, or one of your people dies."

Mita said instantly, "Give us the young girl. She will please Maug better than the small male."

Abbey turned pale, for Mita's long bony finger was pointed directly at her. She could not say a word, but she looked plaintively at Dave.

He spoke up at once. "We will kill this tiger for you, my Queen, and we will do it tomorrow."

Faya looked at him with admiration. "It shall be as you say, but I do not think that you will succeed."

The Sleepers filed out, and as soon as they were outside they saw that a sizable crowd of men had gathered.

"What will you do?" Gaclan asked.

"We will go do battle with the tiger," Josh said.

"Take me with you," Gaelan begged. "I can pull a bow as well as most."

"No, this is something that we must do for ourselves, although I thank you for your offer."

Gaelan looked disappointed but said no more.

Then Rolf walked up. "I will go with you, although I am no warrior."

Josh said warmly, "That is a wonderful thing—that you would be willing to risk your life for strangers."

"I think we are more than that," Rolf said. "We are friends, aren't we?"

"I'd like to think so," Josh said, and he took the prince's hand. "But you know your mother would never permit it. It's almost certain death the way they tell it, but we have faith in Goél."

These were brave words, and a hum of admiration went around the men of the village. The Sleepers heard more than one man say, "These are bold young people, indeed! They are warriors themselves."

However, when the boys were inside the hut where they were to sleep before the tiger hunt in the morning, Josh was not so confident.

"Tell us about that tiger," he said to Reb and Wash.

Reb was usually not afraid of anything, but he was respectful as he said, "He's a big varmint, Josh. He runs faster than a race horse, and if we miss, we're dead. That woman got off one arrow. Why, he killed her before you could bat an eye! She never had a chance."

"But there'll be five of us," Josh said. "Surely one of us can get an arrow in him."

"We better," Wash said slowly. "He's a mighty big old tiger—and what's more, I got an idea there's more than one of him."

"What do you mean by that?" Josh demanded.

"I mean he's got a mate, ain't he? I don't know whether that was a male or a female, since he wasn't wearing skirts or pants, but where there's a male there's a female, and where there's a female there's a male. Ain't that so, Reb?"

"I think Wash may be right, which makes it twice as bad."

"Well, we've got to do it, no matter what it is. So we ask for our weapons, we sharpen our arrows, we make sure our bowstrings aren't frayed, we get our swords in shape, and then we sleep."

Dave nodded slowly. "That's right, Josh. We'll do all we can do. That's all Goél's ever asked of us."

At the name of Goél, the room seemed to grow warmer, and Josh felt his presence in a strange way.

After they'd gone to bed, he heard Wash whisper to Jake, "You know, I just sort of feel like Goél is right here with us."

"Yeah, I know. I feel the same thing. I'm scared a little bit, but not as scared as if I didn't feel like Goél was going with us somehow. I wonder how he does that?"

"I guess he's just Goél. He helps them what believes in him, and I sure think we better believe in him tomorrow."

At daybreak Gaelan saw that the entire village was up to see the Sleepers as they prepared to leave. The seven all carried weapons. Their swords were sharp as knives after being treated all night. Each shouldered a quiverful of arrows with razor-sharp tips, and they all had put on new bowstrings.

As they started to march out, Gaelan noticed Princess Merle, standing near the gate beside her father. He moved closer to her and said, "They look pretty good, don't they, Princess?"

Merle stared at him. She swallowed hard and said, "Yes, they do."

"I offered to go with them, but they said this was something they had to do for themselves."

"Why—why did you offer to do that? They're all going to be killed."

"They are my friends. And the small woman, I feel sorry for her."

"You really would be willing to risk your life for Abbey?"

"Why wouldn't I risk it for a fellow human being? You'd do the same, wouldn't you?"

Merle stared at him for a moment longer, then shook her head slightly. "I never risk anything for anybody," she said bitterly.

"That's too bad," Gaelan said, surprised that he had seen emotion in this girl he'd thought to be so hard. "Maybe they'll make it back. I hope so."

"So do I," Merle murmured.

He saw that she was tremendously moved. "I'm surprised to see you take it so hard. I didn't know you felt like that about things."

"I guess I have feelings like everybody else."

"I see that now. You never showed them to me before."

Merle whispered, "I didn't know I had them myself."

She walked away.

Gaelan thought, *She's got a heart behind all that armor. I'm surprised to see it.*

"Spread out now," Reb said. He was leading the group as they approached the timber where the tiger had disappeared. "Don't get close together. If we're in a clump, he might get us all. But if we're spread out, he can only run at one at a time. Everybody watch him, and don't shoot too soon. As a matter of fact, you remember what that soldier said on Bunker Hill during the American Revolution?"

134

"He said, 'Don't give up the ship,' didn't he?" Jake grinned.

"No, he didn't! He said, 'Don't shoot until you see the whites of their eyes.'"

"That wouldn't make any sense," Jake argued. "Some people could see better than others. They could see the whites of their eyes half a mile away, some couldn't see 'em ten feet, and some of the eyes wasn't as white as others either. Why, they'd have been shooting all over the place. That's dumb!"

"Well, that tiger doesn't have anything but meanness in *his* eyes, and he'll be on you before you know it. So don't get in a hurry. Better one arrow well shot than two that miss."

"What if two tigers come at the same time?"

"Then everybody to the right of Jake there, you take the one on the right. Those of us over here will take the one on the left."

"Do we shoot for the head?" Josh asked.

"No," Reb said quickly, "that's too hard a shot. I'm telling you that thing moves like a freight train! He's almost as big too. Try to hit him right in the chest. That won't kill him, but it'll slow him down. And when he slows down, we can drive some more arrows home. It would take a pretty good shot to hit him in the heart, which is the only thing that'll stop him. All right, let's go."

Then he halted and said, "By the way, in case this doesn't turn out too good for old Reb—" he grinned broadly "—I want to tell you, you been a good bunch of cowboys. I'm right proud to have been one of you."

"That goes for me too," Josh said.

And all of them bashfully spoke their last farewells —or what might be their last words.

The grass was waist high, and they knew that the tiger could be hidden until they were very close.

"Watch for any grass moving," Josh said.

Even as he spoke, Wash said, "Look. Over there. To the right. I think I saw something."

Sure enough, though there was no wind, and most of the grass was standing still, off to the right a small section of it was moving.

"Heads up," Reb said. "I think—" He broke off and yelled, "Here he comes!" He gave his Rebel yell, then drew back his bow to a full pull.

Every eye was on the tiger charging the right side of their line. But then, almost immediately, another tiger sprang up and charged the left.

"Remember," Reb yelled, "we'll take this one—you guys on the right take the first one."

The tigers seemed to double in size with every leap. It was impossible to get a steady bead as they bounded forward, but Reb managed to cry, "Hold on, now. Let him get closer!" And then he yelled, *"Now!"*

The tiger to the left was no more than thirty feet away, charging straight at Reb.

He released his arrow and reached over his shoulder to get another. He knew he would never have time to beat the speed of the tiger, but he vowed to die trying. He saw his first arrow strike the tiger low in the chest. The beast faltered and missed a step. Then another arrow took him, this time low in the flank, and Josh yelled, "I got him!"

But Reb was not listening. He fitted another arrow.

The tiger was no more than ten feet away and still charging when Reb released his second arrow. He did not have time to see where it went, for he was bowled over. He smelled rank cat smell and ducked his head as the animal swerved. He expected to feel the gigantic teeth crunching on him at any time and thought himself no better than dead.

A mighty blow struck his shoulder. He went rolling in the dirt, but he held onto his bow despite the pain. When he came to his feet, the tiger was clawing vainly at an arrow that had struck him in the throat. Quickly Reb notched an arrow and, ignoring the pain in his shoulder, drew a careful bead. This arrow struck the beast in the left side, right behind the foreleg. The tiger turned to snap it but then fell, clawing at the ground.

"We got him!" Jake yelled. "We got him!"

Reb turned then to the right and saw the other tiger mauling one of the Sleepers, and his heart lurched. He saw also that several arrows had penetrated the animal's hide. "Come on," he yelled, "let's put that one down!"

Jake and Wash were quickly fitting arrows. And then Reb realized that it was Josh who was being mauled. He uttered another Rebel yell as he notched an arrow and ran in close.

The tiger saw him and released the limp form of Josh, which flopped like a rag and fell to the ground.

Coolly Reb drew his bowstring back, and when the huge beast opened his mouth, he let the arrow fly. His heart gave a leap as the arrow struck the tiger directly in the open mouth. Other arrows penetrated him, and soon he lay still.

Reb threw down his bow and ran to Josh. He saw that his friend's shirt was bloodied, and he pulled him up to a sitting position. Jerking the shirt back, he saw four bleeding furrows across the boy's chest.

"Are you all right, Josh? You're not going to die on me, are you?"

137

Josh made a face and looked down at his bloody chest. "No, but I was ready to quit before he was."

Reb laughed and hugged him. "You son of a gun," he said, "let's get that bleeding stopped. We gotta wash that out. Them tiger claws is bound to have poison in them."

"You got clawed yourself. Look at your shoulder there," Dave said, running up. "Here, let's get both of you cleaned up."

He opened their small kit of medical supplies and carefully dressed the wounds of the two boys, while Wash stood over one of the dead tigers.

"I wish we had us a camera. I'd like to cut his old head off and mount it on the wall," Wash cried.

"I imagine we'll get the skins. I never saw such beasts," Jake said. "Let's go back and tell 'em that the Sleepers have done produced."

Dave pulled out the knife that Josh had given him for his birthday and opened it. It caught the sun as he marched over and proceeded to cut the tails off the two dead animals. "And here's proof," he said. "Can you fellows make it?"

"Sure," Josh and Reb said at once. They were on their feet now, although both of them were pale. "Let's go back and show those women what men can do."

The victory of the Sleepers over the tigers shook the village as nothing short of an earthquake could have shaken it.

When they came back carrying their trophies, the village men ignored the cries of the women and rushed out to where the tigers lay. They skinned the beasts, and now the pelts were posted on the walls of the stockade. The heads were mounted on sharpened stakes. And the village hummed with talk.

138

Ettore and her mother, Marden, viewed all this with distaste. "It looks like Mita's not going to get her sacrifice," Ettore said bitterly. "I wouldn't have cared if the whole bunch of them had gotten killed. They're going to be nothing but trouble."

"Don't worry. We'll see that they don't survive the battle that's coming. We'll instruct some of our best archers to make sure they don't survive."

After the victory celebration and feast, Josh and Dave quietly passed the word so that a number of the men came to meet with the Sleepers secretly. Among them, to everyone's surprise, was Rolf.

Josh turned to him when all the men were gathered. "Rolf, I don't want to be unkind, but maybe you don't need to be at this meeting."

"Why not, Josh?"

"Because things are going to happen, and you may not like some of them."

Rolf was a quick-thinking young man. "I know what you're planning," he said calmly. "You think it's wrong for the women to rule the village the way they do."

"That's right," Dave answered before Josh could speak. "And I have nothing against your mother. She's been a good queen, but she's sick, and she's not able to lead anymore. And your sister is not able either. And there are some power hungry people out there. That means that sooner or later someone will kill her to get the throne."

Rolf's mind probably had already gone over this territory many times. "I know you're right," he said, "but are there men who could do what the women have been doing?"

"You know your family," Josh said. "We all know

your father is a very wise man. He's not a warrior—but no one expects the king to go out and fight. He has a war chief to do that. I think you could find a war chief right here in Gaelan—or you yourself could be a warrior." He looked about at the men and said, "You haven't had training, but most of you could learn. Are you willing?"

A hum of talk went around. One of the smaller men said, "I'm not as big as the warrior maids. I have not had the training they have, and there's not time to learn . . ."

"That's where Goél comes in," Josh said. "Let me tell you about him—how he can give power to them who have no power."

Eagerly the men crowded forward. For a long time that night, Josh spoke of Goél. He spoke also of the power of love. He explained how things in the village would have to change.

"It's not might that makes right," he said. "There's a need for gentleness and consideration of other people in this world. In our situation, you men have those qualities more than the women, but they can learn."

"Yes," Rolf said at once, and a sad smile came to his lips. "It will be hard for them, but they can learn."

14
Lesson for a Princess

For several days little was heard in the village but talk of the death of the tigers.

The status of Mita, the medicine woman, had plunged. She had prophesied that the tigers would kill any of the Sleepers who came against them; now that her prophecy had failed, she had become almost a comic figure. The villagers had long been frightened of her. But now they felt that whatever powers she had had died with the tigers, and they merely laughed at her.

The Sleepers themselves found that the deed had done much to raise their status. Even Ettore kept her hands and her cane off Josh, for which he was grateful.

Sarah had whispered, "I think she's actually afraid of us now. Anybody that could kill a tiger could certainly kill a woman like her—although we wouldn't, of course."

Rolf had changed so greatly that his parents grew worried about him.

"What's troubling you, son?" Chava asked.

The young man was sitting underneath a shade tree, simply staring into space. He had been shelling beans. Now suddenly he looked down with distaste at the unshelled beans and then up at his father. "I'm not happy, Father," he said.

"That's obvious." Chava sat down, and they talked.

Chava was wise. He knew better than to ask directly if Rolf was caught up in the movement of the men. He himself had seen the tide flowing in that direction, and he feared there would be bloodshed before it was over. He had a daughter who would fight to the death because of her pride; and now this son of his, who had never lifted his hand against anyone, seemed to be on a head-on-collision course with her and the warrior maids.

"I don't know what to do," Rolf said finally. "Tell me what to do, Father."

"You're a man, my son. I have not been, perhaps, a good adviser for you. I've been content to take my place and to help your mother."

Rolf looked up and smiled. "You've always loved my mother. I've always known that."

"Yes, I have. Many times I have wished she were not queen. It's been unhappy and hard for her, and I've done what I could to ease her pain. But things can't stay as they are for long. The men have had a taste of what achievement is like, and they are not going to forget it."

Rolf stared at him. He probably had suspected that his father would not tell him directly what to do. "I wish I were as wise as you," he said.

"Wisdom comes with seeking it—and with age. You already have more wisdom than you think. You also have a gentleness in you that would be good for any woman to know, and you will someday find one to lavish your heart on. But first, perhaps, there will come a harder time."

He said no more, but he thought they understood each other thoroughly.

Gaelan had a conversation that same day with Abbey. He rather admired the young woman and found her easy to talk to.

142

Abbey said, before they had spoken long, "Josh told me you offered to go fight the tiger to save my life. I've never thanked you for that."

"No need thanking me. I didn't go. They wouldn't let me."

"But you offered. That's what's important. It was good of you, Gaelan, and I thank you for it."

"I like to think you would have done the same for me, Abbey."

"I don't know—I'm really a coward at heart."

"I don't believe that."

"I'm not like the others."

"You're certainly not like Princess Merle. She's got a tiger's heart."

Abbey glanced at him quickly. "No," she said slowly, "I don't think that's right. She's not as tough and hard as she wants everybody to think."

"Well, she puts on a good act then! I can still feel where she beat me with that cane of hers."

"You've been beaten before, but her latest beating hurt worse than the rest, and I know why."

"What do you mean?"

"It hurt you because you like her more than you want to admit."

"Like her? She's made my life a misery! Of course, she is pretty enough, but—"

"Pretty? Why, she's one of the most beautiful girls you've ever seen, and you know it."

Gaelan's face turned red. "All right, so she's pretty. So what? She can be mean as a snake when she wants to."

Abbey shook her head. "I know, but underneath she's got a sweetness in her. It's just buried under all that stuff about fighting and killing and what she's been brought up to be. If you took a puppy and brought him

143

up to be mean, you couldn't wholly blame the dog, could you? It was his upbringing."

"Well, you can't do anything about a bad dog."

"But you *can* about a young woman. She just needs someone to tell her some things."

"What do you want me to do—quote poetry to her? That's what her father does to her mother, I've heard."

"It wouldn't hurt you."

"Oh, I can't write a poem."

"You don't have to write a poem. Girls don't expect that unless their boyfriends are poets, but they do like to be told sweet things. Why don't you try it?"

"She'd shoot me with an arrow right in the head!"

Abbey smiled. "I don't think so. I think she's just waiting to be told that she's pretty and sweet and that she's appreciated. Try it. See what happens."

"Not me," Gaelan said firmly, pulling his lips into a straight line. "I'm not going to make a fool of myself!"

And he didn't, at least not that day. The next day, however, he was standing outside the house watching some birds circle overhead when he turned quickly at a sound and saw that Princess Merle had come outside. She would have gone by him, but he stopped her, saying, "Look up there. Wouldn't it be nice to fly like those fellows?"

Merle had not spoken to Gaelan except of necessity. She stopped and looked up. "Why, I suppose so."

"I'll bet your father could write a poem about those birds and the way they move. See how smooth they are? They don't waste their strength beating the air. Look at them glide! Wouldn't that be nice to just soar around like that?"

"I think it would, but of course we could never do that."

144

"The Sleepers did."

Now he had her attention. "What do you mean, the Sleepers did?" she demanded.

"They were in a country where men flew like birds. Didn't they tell you about that?"

"No, tell me."

"Well, you'll have to get Sarah or Abbey, or maybe Dave, to tell you. They were all there." He related as best he could the story of the birdmen of the desert and how the Sleepers themselves had been fitted with wings and learned to soar on the updrafts.

"Must be great," he said. "I'd like to go to that place sometime."

"It's very far away, isn't it?"

"I guess so, but I'm young. I intend to see some of the world while I've got a chance."

A peace had come over the village, a quiet, and Princess Merle stood for some time listening as Gaelan told her about some of the places he had heard about.

Suddenly he said, "You know, Princess, I've gotten angry enough at you a few times that I wanted to strangle you."

She looked startled.

Gaelan fixed his eyes on her. He seemed to have trouble speaking but finally said, "But I know that you're not as hard as you pretend to be."

"What makes you think I'm not?" she snapped.

"I just know it," he said simply. "For one thing, you were frightened when the Sleepers went out to fight the tiger. That's when I saw you had . . . well . . . gentleness in you, and I liked it. It's something I like to see in a woman. Sarah has a lot of that, and Abbey too."

"Gentleness is a weakness."

"No, it isn't. Your father is gentle, and he's not weak. I think even your mother has a gentleness. She

145

doesn't show it much, but I bet she shows it to you."

Reluctantly, Merle said, "Yes, she does, and Father certainly does."

"I think I admire them more than any older people I ever saw. You're lucky to have them for parents. And that brother of yours. Why, he's got all kinds of good qualities. He's got gentleness in him too, but he's strong."

"Rolf? I suppose so."

"I know I'm just a servant, but I'm going to tell you something." He set his feet as if he were expecting a blow and put his hands behind him, grasping them firmly.

Puzzled, she turned fully to face him. "What is it?" she asked.

"You're the prettiest girl I ever saw," he said, "and I think under all that warrior stuff you've probably got a kind streak in you." When he had said this, Gaelan waited and was astonished to see the face of the princess of the Fedorians turn pale. He said quickly, "I—I didn't mean to insult you." She still did not speak, so he shrugged and said, "Well, it's the truth. You *are* pretty." He turned and walked off.

If Gaelan had struck her in the face, Princess Merle could not have been more shocked. Yet she realized she was not angry. Instead she felt warmth and pleasure spread through her. She reached up and touched her face and found it glowing. No one had ever told her she was pretty—and certainly not that she was kind. Slowly she walked back into the house and found her mother.

"What is it, Merle? You look pale. Don't you feel well?"

146

"Gaelan told me I was pretty, and—he said I was kind on the inside."

A gleam of humor came to the queen's eyes. "He's got good eyes. You've kept that kind streak covered up pretty well, blustering around—as I taught you to do, of course—and anybody could have told you you were pretty. You can see yourself in the mirror, can't you?"

"I know, but it was different when he said it. Mother, I feel so funny lately. What's wrong with me?"

The queen reached out and pulled her daughter forward. She held her to her breast tightly and said, "You're becoming a woman, Merle. Sometimes that's a little painful, but when a young man like that tells you you're pretty and kind, it makes you feel . . . different."

"I don't know *what* to feel like. I'm all confused."

"I felt the same way when I was your age, but I'm glad to see it happen. I want my girl to be a woman, not just a warrior maid. I wish," she said slowly, "I'd had the chance to be that. It would have meant a great deal to your father."

Later, Merle hunted up Sarah. She had recovered, at least outwardly, from the shock of Gaelan's compliment. For a long time she talked with Sarah about unimportant things. At last she cleared her throat and said as innocently as she could, "Sarah, how old are you?"

"I'm sixteen."

"Then—did Josh or any boy ever tell you you were pretty?"

"Josh has—and one or two others." Sarah smiled suddenly. "I liked it too, even though I didn't always believe it. As long as *they* did, that was all I needed."

"Why did it make you feel so good to be told that?"

"I think most of us feel a little insecure. Even the prettiest girls feel that. We had a thing called beauty contests back in my world—"

"What was that?"

"Oh, the girls all paraded around, and judges decided which one was the prettiest."

"Did you ever win?"

"Oh, no!" Sarah laughed. "I never even entered a beauty contest. I would not have won."

"I bet you would have. Tell me about it."

"Well, the strange thing is that the girls who won the beauty contests—I knew several of them—they never were satisfied. *They* didn't feel they were pretty, even though the judges had said so. They always went around trying to buy prettier clothes and trying to fix their hair different, and they never felt that a boy liked them just for themselves."

She went on talking for some time about her limited experience with beauty contestants, and then she asked directly, "Has some young man been telling you you're pretty?"

Merle considered denying it, but then she whispered, "Why, yes, one did."

"I admire his judgment. You are a very pretty girl. You're pretty spoiled, though."

Merle's eyes flashed for a moment, then she laughed shortly. "I know. I've always had everything I've wanted, and now—"

When the girl broke off, Sarah said, "Now you're not sure you want those things anymore."

"Yes. Why is that?"

"I think it's because there's an emptiness in all the women of your tribe. They've given up everything to be fighters, and they've put aside softness and gentleness, and that's what a woman is, really. We're different from men. Of course, we're different physically, but we're different inside too."

"How are we different inside?" Merle was fasci-

148

nated by all this. She had never heard anything like it.

"Well, boys are sort of matter-of-fact. For instance, if I asked Josh what he did, he just gives me the big picture, and I'll say, 'I want to hear the little things, the fine print—tell me every detail.' But he doesn't like to do that. Women like things like that, and they like to be told nice, sweet little things. Josh is learning, and I'm teaching him how to talk like that."

"How can you teach him?"

"Oh, there are ways." Sarah smiled enigmatically. "I'll tell you some of them."

Sarah talked and Merle listened, and soon the two girls were giggling together.

Sarah thought, *It's almost like a slumber party at home. This girl is a princess, and she's been a warrior and probably killed people in battle, but she doesn't know as much as a ninth grader back in Oldworld. And really she's sweet underneath all that warrior stuff.*

When Merle left, Sarah put her arms around her and kissed her on the cheek. "I'll keep your secret."

"What secret?"

"The secret about who told you you were pretty."

"You *know?*"

"I can make a good guess. He is certainly a fine-looking young man. Any girl would be proud to have his admiration."

Merle stared at her.

Walking home, Merle thought, *I don't know much about life or boys—or anything!*

Early the next morning Merle was awakened by

149

loud cries. She sat straight up in bed, and what she heard almost froze her blood.

"Ulla is coming! Ulla is coming!"

"Ulla, the chief of the Londos!" She leaped up, looked out the window, and saw the guards assembling. Warrior maidens were hastily grabbing spears and shields. Quickly she dressed and ran to where her father was helping the queen painfully get out of bed.

"Is it war?" Merle asked.

Queen Faya looked at her, her lips pale and her face drawn tense. "Yes," she said, "it's war."

15

Battle Cry

As the regiment of women warriors gathered, Marden and Ettore stood to one side.

Marden said, "Remember the plan now. Ulla will come straight down through the valley. The queen will be right in the middle of it, surrounded by a few of her warriors, but she cannot survive his attack."

"And as soon as the queen—and the princess—go down, that will be the sign for us to attack on the flanks."

"Exactly." Marden chuckled deep in her throat. "We will be queens before this day is over!"

"And we will rule well, won't we, Mother?"

The two laughed together.

In the queen's house, Chava assisted his wife into her armor. His face was sad, and he said, "You do not have to do this, Faya."

"Shall I lie at home on a bed while my warriors go to face death?"

"Let others go who are younger," he pleaded. "I cannot spare you."

His plea almost forced Faya to change her mind, but she knew this was one thing she must do.

Chava said, "You cannot win. The army is too small. You nearly lost last time, and this time the odds are even greater."

"Then we will die with honor." She put a hand out to him, and he took it. She held it for a moment, searching his face, and finally whispered, "I would regret leaving you and the children—but I must go."

Chava helped her to the door, where a litter waited for her. When she had seated herself in it, some of the stronger men picked up the four handles and carried her to where the troops were assembled.

The queen surveyed the ranks of women warriors, and pride came to her—but sadness as well. She knew that before the sun went down many of them would be dead and others would be maimed. She did not feel in her heart that she could win this battle. Chava had spoken truly. Her army *was* too small, and she knew well that Ulla had a mighty force on the way.

Nevertheless, she roused herself and said, "Warrior maids, we go to fight for the honor of the House of Fedor."

The Amazons raised their spears and shook their shields, and the morning air was rent with their shrill cries. There was no fear in them, Faya saw, and she was proud again of their strength and their courage. She continued, saying, "Many of us will not see another sun; but if we die, we die for the honor of Fedor." Again there were cheers, and she waited until they died down. "The enemy is powerful, and we are few, but we will fight as we have fought before."

"Queen Mother!"

Every eye turned to Rolf.

The queen's son held in his hand a bow, and on his back was a quiver. His eyes were fixed on his mother, and his face was tense. Rolf wore no armor, but there was a boldness about him, and he looked strong and able. "I will go with you to fight this battle, and many other of our men will go with us."

Mutters of disbelief ran through the ranks.

"This cannot be. Men do not fight!" Marden cried out, shaking her shield.

"Why do they not fight?" Rolf said. "I can shoot as straight as you, Marden. I could beat you with a sword right now. I am stronger and faster than you. If you do not believe, come and I will prove it."

If Rolf had commanded the sun to disappear, the crowd could not have appeared more shocked.

Chava came to stand beside his wife, and he put his hand on her shoulder. "Let the boy go," he whispered. "He is a man. He must fight for his home and for his people."

"Must it be so, Chava?" Queen Faya asked. She suddenly realized that she might lose both son and daughter in the battle, but one look at her son's face told her that indeed it must be so. She lifted her voice and said, "Let it be so then, my son. You shall fight beside your mother."

"I will go too."

Everyone turned to see Gaelan, who had procured a sword and waved it in the air. "I am a slave here, yet I will fight for the tribe. You will not find me behind when the battle starts."

One by one, men stepped forward. Some had found old swords. Some bore spears, some bows. They did not look military.

The queen looked them over with shock. She could not speak for a moment.

Cries rose from Marden and Ettore. "Refuse the men. It would shame us," Ettore said, "to let the weak men go."

"Try us!" a man shouted and lifted his sword. "We will fight for our homes as well as you."

"Let us go, my Queen," another cried, "and fight for you as true men!"

A cry went up then from all the men, pledging their allegiance and their love for the queen. No one had done this before, and Chava, holding his wife's hand, whispered, "Let them go. Let them be men."

This decided Queen Faya. She held up a hand, and when silence came she said, "We will all fight as one. Together we may be able to defeat the foe. Forward, now, into the battle."

The Sleepers had armed themselves and were at the front of the ranks. The queen went on before, being carried on her litter. Warrior maids flanked her on both sides and walked in orderly ranks behind.

"It looks like we're going right into that valley," Josh said, motioning ahead with his bow. "Seems like a good place for an ambush to me."

Reb looked up at the sides of the ravine. "I think that's where we're supposed to ambush Ulla. At least that's what I heard the queen say. It seems she got word that he's coming to meet us right there. Looks about like the place where we took Ulla before. I hope they send scouts out."

"I think they have. Not all the warrior maids are here," Dave said. He looked over the men, and a worried look crossed his face. "The men are eager enough, but they just haven't had any training. We'll have to lead them as best we can. There're some good men in this army, though."

"Yes, there are," Josh said. "Let's divide them up into squads. We can handle them better that way."

The men marched in three groups, commanded by Josh, Reb, and Dave. The tall Sleepers towered above the others, so that they were easy to see. The squads kept in reasonably straight order, and finally they were in the center of the valley.

"There comes Ulla, and he has a host with him!" Queen Faya said.

The maids spread out in a line ahead of the queen, but their ranks looked very thin.

Faya asked, "Where are the rest of the warrior maids?"

"On the flanks," Marden said. "I will see to them. Come, Ettore."

When they were gone, Merle said, "You're not well enough protected here, Mother. They've left us with very few warriors."

"I know—I feel something has gone wrong."

Merle was suddenly afraid, not for herself but for her mother. She saw that the ranks of the warrior maids were thin indeed. Looking back, she saw Dave, and she ran to him.

"Dave," she said, "my mother! She cannot survive the attack! Will you help with your men?"

"Of course, Princess." He turned to Gaelan. "Take half of our men over to the right. I'll take the other half to the left. We'll form a circle around the queen. It'll be hot, but we can stand it."

Gaelan smiled as he passed close to the princess and whispered, "I still say you're pretty." Then he was gone.

The battle took form almost at once. It was good, indeed, that the men had come, for when Ulla's troops struck, they struck hard. Arrows flew, and there were screams from the wounded and dying.

The Sleepers commanded their companies well. Sarah stood beside Josh, loosing arrow after arrow into the masked men that rushed toward her. They were tattooed and horrible-looking, but she did not

155

flinch. Beside her, some of the warrior maids were falling, and she entreated Goél for help.

Merle was in the midst of the battle, staying close to her mother. She cut down three of Ulla's warriors, and then two attacked her at the same time. She saw that she could not survive and prepared to die.

Then suddenly a form flashed by her, and one of her attackers fell. Gaelan had come to her aid. He was battling like a wild man with his sword.

Merle leaped to his side, and together the two drove Ulla's men back.

Still Ulla had the superiority.

"I don't think we can hold them," Josh said.

Reb yelled, "Look! There comes help! We got 'em trapped!" as fresh troops of warrior maids rushed down from the sides of the hills. They struck Ulla's men on the right and left flank so that they had only one direction to go, and that was backward. Some of the enemy fought their way out, but most of them finally threw down their swords and pleaded for mercy.

"It's a victory," Princess Merle called and held her sword high. "Throw your weapons down and surrender."

Ulla himself had been badly wounded and could not command his warriors. They were now surrounded on all four sides, and the victory belonged to the women—and the men—of Fedor.

Princess Merle had taken a wound on her right arm. She was bleeding and beginning to feel faint, but she went to her mother. "Are you all right?" she asked.

"Yes, but you're wounded."

"I'll take care of that, Your Majesty." It was Gaelan who stripped off his shirt, made a bandage, and stanched the bleeding. "Are you all right?" he asked the princess anxiously.

Merle looked up into his hazel eyes, weakness took her, and she felt herself swaying. "I might need a little help," she said faintly. She felt him pick her up like a child, and she laid her head on his chest. "Take me home, please, Gaelan," she whispered.

"Yes, I will take you home—and I still think you're the prettiest girl I ever saw."

It was a weary group that made its way back to the village.

"We will return and tend to our wounded. Keep the prisoners close," the queen said, "but harm none of them."

That night there was a victory celebration that the village never forgot. There were heroes aplenty, including Rolf and Gaelan and Princess Merle, not to mention all of the Seven Sleepers.

Later Chava said to his wife gently, "I think things are going to change a great deal in Fedor."

Queen Faya lay back and half closed her eyes. She smiled and said, "Yes, and I think it's time they did change."

16
Long Live the King!

The village set about healing and caring for its wounded. The battle had taken a high toll among the warrior maids. And everyone recognized that the men had turned the tide. They had been untrained, but their courage and steadfastness had spoken for itself.

Marden felt defeated because her plan had failed and the queen lived, but she felt sure that would soon change. "She can't live long," she whispered confidently to Ettore, "and we can always be sure that something happens to that daughter of hers. It's not too late yet."

The queen herself said little publicly, but she talked for long hours with her husband. And then the word came forth that the queen had commanded a royal assembly.

Every person who could walk came, and those who could not walk begged to be carried. The meeting ground was filled with anxious heroes. The Sleepers stood over to one side, curious as to what the queen would say.

Queen Faya hobbled out on her crutch, aided by her husband and her son, and took her throne. Then the two men stepped back slightly, and Princess Merle took her place beside her brother.

"My people, you have fought valiantly, and your queen thanks you." She went over the rolls of the dead, and honor was done them. Then she lifted her head and said, "I am no longer able to rule over you . . ."

Marden and Ettore looked at each other with anticipation. "Soon we won't have her to contend with," Ettore whispered with satisfaction.

The queen spoke of the burden of leading the people. Then she said, "If it had not been for the men, we would all be the slaves of Ulla. Is this not so?"

A mutter went through the ranks of the women, but the men said, "You are our queen."

"I will still be your queen," she said, "but things will be different from now on in the land of Fedor." She looked over the ranks of women warriors, and her voice carried clearly on the morning air. "As long as any of us can remember, a queen has ruled over our people. Some of you may think what I am going to do is wrong, but I think it is wisdom. When I was a young woman, I wanted glory as much as any of you warrior maids. It was what I was taught, even as you were taught. But now that I grow older I begin to see that there is something wrong with a system that makes warriors out of women. From this day forth you will have a king."

A cry went up from the warrior maids, but Faya held up her hands. "Peace—hear me out!"

She turned to her husband and said tenderly, "For many years, the decisions have mostly been made by Chava, as my adviser. It was his wisdom that has kept us from being devoured by our neighbors. He never spoke loudly, but he has never given me bad advice. Now he will be the king, and I name our son, Rolf, as heir to the throne!"

Pandemonium broke out.

Marden cried, "No! We will fight before we will have a *king.*"

Then Marden felt the point of a sword against her back, and she stiffened.

Chava had done his work well. He had warned all the men, and Marden and her daughter were immediately surrounded by men whose bright swords glittered in the morning sunlight. The queen was speaking again, and Marden was forced to listen.

"And now your royal king will speak." She turned to her husband.

Chava stepped forward. He wore a simple white robe, and he spoke quietly. "Men and women, we need each other. We cannot do without one another. We have heard much of how men and women worked together and loved one another in the land of the Seven Sleepers. They will be our teachers. They will teach us of Goél, who knows the ways of love. We will no more be frightened of Maug, for he will be banished from our land."

He spoke on with great eloquence. After he finished and stepped back, Dave yelled, "Long live the king! Long live King Chava of Fedor!"

The air rang with the sound of cheering, and even some of the women joined in.

After Chava was crowned and officially given his new office, the crowd broke up.

Princess Merle turned to her brother and looked at him with new eyes. "I never thought of you as being a king, but you will be one day, my brother."

"We will see if I am worthy," Rolf said. His eyes were following a young man who was walking toward them. "I think someone wants to speak to you."

Startled, Merle saw that Gaelan was coming straight for her. Rolf faded away, and she stood stock-still, wondering what Gaelan would say.

He had one hand behind his back. Suddenly he brought it out and presented her with a beautiful bouquet of red and white flowers. "For you," he said. He looked a little embarrassed. "Sarah said this is what young men do who admire young women. Will you accept them?"

Princess Merle took the bouquet. She buried her face in it to hide her confusion, then she looked up and whispered, "They're very beautiful, Gaelan. Thank you."

"Will you walk with me down by the river? There are things I would say to you where it's quiet and peaceful."

"I will go with you."

Queen Faya was watching. She reached out and took her husband's hand, saying, "I think we will be seeing a great deal of that young man."

"There are worse young men in the world to have for a son-in-law," he replied quietly.

The Sleepers stayed in Fedor for several weeks, training the villagers as best they could. They explained the nature of Goél and how a battle would soon come when all the good and true people of Nuworld would have to stand against the powers of darkness. Teaching the people was easy, for the Fedorians were tired of Maug and the sacrifices he demanded. And Mita left the village with several of her cronies, so that her shrill voice was heard no more.

But the day finally came to say good-bye. Their knapsacks were full, their weapons were bright, and the entire village lined up to wish the Seven Sleepers farewell.

The Sleepers all knelt before the king and queen, who blessed them, and when they rose, they shook hands with as many people as they could. Princess Merle was there to hug the two girls, and the tall form of Gaelan was by her side. He shook hands with the young men and said, "We will meet again."

Then it was all over, and they left.

For several hours the Sleepers traveled hard, hoping to make good time before sunset. All of them felt drained, and they made camp early. As they sat around the fire eating, they talked about the return journey to Daybright's ship.

Afterward, Dave said, "Abbey, would you like to go look at the river for a minute?"

Abbey looked at him with surprise, but she nodded. "Why, yes, I think I would."

They walked along the riverbank for a long time. Sometimes they were silent, sometimes they talked about what had happened in Fedor. They finally sat down on an old log.

The rising moon was bright and illuminated the river. The water glittered as it flowed past, the little ripples seeming to wave at them. They talked awhile about home, and then they fell silent again.

After a while she said, "Dave—"

"Yes, what is it, Abbey?"

"I guess I've had to learn another lesson. It seems like I'm so dumb! I'll never get everything learned."

"You're not dumb." He took her hand and held it with both of his big ones. It felt small and soft and defenseless. He saw that she was troubled, and he moved closer and put an arm around her. "What's the matter? Tell me about it. We're friends, aren't we?"

"Oh, Dave, I was so wrong to talk about women needing to boss men. I see how awful that was."

"You made a mistake, but so did I. Men aren't to boss women around either. I can see that."

"Then how do we get along?"

163

"Why, we work together," Dave said.

Then he started to tell Abbey how he had learned to treasure things he saw in her that he had never noticed before.

Listening, she turned her face toward him.

He was surprised at how large her eyes seemed, and he knew that she had been using her cosmetics, for she smelled faintly of perfume. "When you grow up," he said, "I'll have a few more things to say to you."

"I was sixteen yesterday," she said. "Is that grown-up enough? I'm sixteen, and you're seventeen."

"I think," Dave said huskily, "that's just about right." He bent his head and kissed her.

Josh and Sarah had been sitting in the shadows on the riverbank when Dave and Abbey approached. They turned their heads away as the two kissed, and when Dave and Abbey got up and left, Sarah said, "We're nothing but accidental Peeping Toms."

"I know. It's bad, isn't it?" Josh said. "I probably won't ever do this again—not until the next time."

Then Sarah said, "Didn't I tell you about those two? I knew they fought so much they'd eventually fall in love."

Josh put his arm around her. "I don't understand much about romance. How does a fellow go about it?"

"What do you mean, how does a fellow go about it?"

"I mean, do you take lessons? You've read lots of romances. I've never read any of those things." His arm tightened, and he said, "What does a fellow do?"

"I think you're doing plenty right now," Sarah said sharply.

"Did I ever tell you how pretty you are, Sarah?"

"Don't try to get around me, Josh Adams."

Josh said, "I wrote a poem for you."

"You did? Oh, Josh, let me hear it!"

It was a very bad poem, but when he was through she sighed and put her head against his shoulder.

"Oh, Josh, that's the most beautiful poem I ever heard in my life."

"I've got lots more poems in me." He pulled her closer. "Here's another one . . ."

Other Titles from Moody Press and Gilbert Morris:

Kerrigan Kids #1

The Kerrigan Kids are headed to Africa to take pictures and write a story on a once fierce tribe. The Kids may be able to travel to Africa but if Duffy can't learn to swallow her pride and appreciate others, they may be left behind with their dreaded Aunt Minnie!
ISBN #0-8024-1578-4

Kerrigan Kids #2

With a whole countryful of places to explore and exciting new adventures to be had, the Kerrigan Kids can't help but have a good time in England. The Kerrigan Kids also learn an important lesson about having a good attitude and about being a good friend.
ISBN #0-8024-1579-2

Kerrigan Kids #3

After several mishaps including misdirected luggage, the Kerrigans are reminded that bad things can happen to good people and the importance of trusting in God even during difficult circumstances.
ISBN #0-8024-1580-6

Kerrigan Kids #4

The Sunday before they leave, the kids are reminded of the story of the Good Samaritan. When there is no one to meet their two new friends from the plane trip at the airport, the Kerrigan clan puts what they learned about helping other into practice.
ISBN #0-8024-1580-6

A Gilbert Morris Mystery

Join Juliet "Too Smart" Jones and her home-schooled friends as they attempt to solve exciting mysteries (ages 7-12).

1 Too Smart Jones & the Pool Party, 0-8024-4025-8
2 Too Smart Jones & the Buried Jewels, 0-8024-4026-6
3 Too Smart Jones & the Disappearing Dogs, 0-8024-4027-4
4 Too Smart Jones & the Dangerous Woman, 0-8024-4028-2
5 Too Smart Jones & the Stranger in the Cave, 0-8024-4029-0
6 Too Smart Jones & the Cat's Secret, 0-8024-4030-4
7 Too Smart Jones & the Stolen Bicycle, 0-8024-4031-2
8 Too Smart Jones & the Wilderness Mystery, 0-8024-4032-0
9 Too Smart Jones & the Spooky Mansion, 0-8024-4029-0
10 Too Smart Jones & the Mysterious Artist, 0-8024-4034-7

The Lost Chronicles

The Dark Lord has been busy, and once again Goel is sending the Seven Sleepers to spoil his plans. This time Josh and his friends are off to Whiteland, a place of sled dogs and igloos, polar bears and seals (ages 7-12).

#1 The Spell of the Crystal Chair, 0-8024-3667-6
#2 Savage Game of Lord Zarak, 0-8024-3668-4
#3 Strange Creatures of Dr. Korbo, 0-8024-3669-2
#4 City of Cyborgs, 0-8024-3670-6
#5 Temptations of Pleasure Island, 0-8024-3671-4
#6 Victims of Nimbo, 0-8024-3672-2
#7 Terrible Beast of Zor, 0-8024-3673-0